THE DOUBLE DEATH

Jonathan Blake knew he should never have gone back to Dead End, especially when almost the entire population had once tried to kill him. However, there was something in the menacing desolation of the place that drew him back. He met Laura again, and a sprinkling of the men who had shot at him before, but the treasure he went back for was now guarded by a new threat—a dragon from the East whose double trickery was enough to make a man begin to doubt himself and his eyes—and then to drive him mad.

THE DOUBLE DEATH

THE DOUBLE DEATH

by

John Newton Chance

Dales Large Print Books
Long Preston, North Yorkshire,
England.

British Library Cataloguing in Publication Data.

Chance, John Newton
   The double death.

   A catalogue record for this book is
   available from the British Library

   ISBN 1-85389-922-4 pbk

First published in Great Britain by Robert Hale Ltd., 1966

Copyright © 1966 by John Newton Chance

The moral right of the author has been asserted

Published in Large Print 1999 by arrangement with Robert
Hale Ltd.

Dales Large Print is an imprint of
Library Magna Books Ltd.
Printed and bound in Great Britain by
T.J. International Ltd., Cornwall, PL28 8RW.

CHAPTER I

1

They say you should never go back to anywhere. Leave it alone—find other places, make everything new all the time; learn and leave the old places in your memory, a feast of the past for the evenings by the fire. They say the place never looks the same anyway, it's smaller, dirtier, dingier. You just wonder how you ever thought it was as fine as you remember it was. You feel sad, cheated somehow. Back at your old school now they are pygmies where in your day they were the genial giants of character and sporting strength. It's never the same, going back.

I should not have gone back to Dead End. It had sunk me once, and when a place gets me down once it can always do it again, because I am that kind of mug who constantly falls for the same thing over and over again. I am the conjurer's fool, the illusionist's fall-back, the politician's friend. And I keep on at it, as if I owe life a proof that every man is a fool at something.

The first time I went to Dead End they carried me away on a stretcher. This second time I just don't know which way it will be. One thing, it can't be pleasant.

2

Dead End looked the same, for I'd left it only a few weeks. If the hospital had been sooner in retrieving the lead from my poisoned area, I'd have been back before that.

I'd have been back as soon as the police, the secret police and the rest of the probe noses had gone.

Secret police? Didn't you know? They're the branch that works for the Government departments, Security, Defence and that kind of excuse for the secret state chopper. It's the same everywhere, but on the Left they wear uniforms.

What's more, you heard nothing official about Dead End. It was sat on from the start. It wouldn't have been good for the public to know how close they had got to being poisoned off. There's no news any more. Only items that officials leak.

Or perhaps I am depressed because of my present situation.

Coming down through the winding crack in the hills that day the floor of the ancient defence basin looked the same. The hills all round, less uneven than the natural kind, their sides ridged where the prehistoric builders had lumped them up. The grey, dilapidated village of Dead End lurched by the dusty road as before, the inn unpainted and scarred by long years of weather. The quarry in the far corner, which had once been the village industry, and the old Manor House half hidden in its belt of dark trees, all looked the same as they had the first time I had seen them, weeks before.

Now, in the bright clear heat of October, I seemed to see something different. The difference was mental, just knowing that some evil had been taken out of it, for really there was nothing different visible at all.

I had a brief feeling of a shiver going through my stomach as I thought of some evil having been taken away from Dead End. Some. There would be a lot left for me. I had been the single man who had smashed the secret industry of Dead End. Those that remained would remember me.

Jonathan Blake, the bastard who ...

I had a brief terrifying vision of many grey faces, steel eyed, sewing their grim traps tight at the mention of my name.

My bowels quaked as I saw the lurching

cottages and the pub that towered above them. Of course, I sopped myself, it might be different now the law had been and cleaned out a lot of the wild men. It might be. This feeling might be just a reflection of the old feeling I had had when I first came into the valley. Might be. It could be I was still a bit mud-minded after the weeks of being doped up and having people dig around my backbone for that damn bullet. It could be. Only I didn't think it was any of those mights or could be's.

I'm a hot head. I can't wait to find out. I have to shove my fist into the fire right away to find if it's as hot as they say, or as I think.

So I stopped at the pub and got out.

There were a couple of men standing at the reeling fence of a cottage garden. They stared down towards me without moving. A woman hanging up a shirt in a back yard stared, her arms still up to the arc of the line.

It could have been their old suspicion of strangers.

It could have been they knew me. They seemed surprised, shocked even, to see me again.

I turned round and by the old coach that huddled in the inn yard I saw a youth leaning against the wall, staring at me with eyes like currants, shining. For an instant I glanced back at the two men by the fence. I caught one of them with his arm raised, pointing towards me. It was like a still from a film; the immobility seeming to make horror.

It's you, I told myself, you and your crummy, worm-witted mind trying to see things the way you want them, though why you want to get the creeps all the time fails the sanity test.

It may seem funny to put it that way, but just then I did get the idea that the strain after convalescence was making me a bit light-headed.

The bar door was wide open. There was

nobody in the room of the long, polished forms and tables; polished from use rather than any lust for cleanliness. The brass oil lamp hung over them. The counter was different, because there were bottles now and bright labels on them, and even a couple of card advertisements. Before this they had brewed their own beer, and Johnny, the young innkeeper, had bought everything else outside and brought it in on his truck.

Johnny had been local leader of the Big Crime.

I had shot Johnny dead.

There was a strong frightening river of memory rushing through my vitals as I stood there and saw Laura, Johnny's mother, come in through the door behind the counter and stare at me.

She was a gorgeous, lush beauty, about thirty-five, a young starter and a long stayer. Dark, Spanish gyppo type, rich with colour and all kinds of promise, including all the passions.

She stared at me with big dark eyes, her hands slowly stroking her hips.

'You came back,' she said, slowly.

'It would seem,' I said.

She came out through the counter gap, looked at me up and down in a slightly puzzled way, then went to the door and looked out at the bright, sunny morning.

'It's going to be hot,' I said, disliking the silence.

She did not look round.

'What do you want this time?' she said.

'I just came back,' I said.

'You've got a reason.'

'Well, I nearly died here once. I've got a kind of affection for the place. I'm dry, Laura. I see you've got some good beer.'

She turned back. She looked magnificent.

'Since Johnny went,' she said.

'I'd like one of those.' I pointed.

She went quickly behind the counter as if to get something to hit me with. I had the impression she was frightened, and that's when people usually do hit out.

She got a bottle and looked at me. I waited, but she got a glass and poured. I think we both relaxed then.

'You took Linda, too,' she said.

'I didn't take Linda,' I said. 'Linda had to go or she'd have stayed stiff. You know that.'

'She'd better not come back,' said Laura. 'I know that, too.'

'That's a funny way to talk of your daughter,' I said.

'They came early, her and Johnny,' Laura said, looking somewhere through the wall. 'It's no loss now.'

'You won't kill me, then?' I said.

Then suddenly she laughed and so did I.

'Have a drink, Laura,' I said. I knew she did, and she did then. We sat down on a form and looked out of the open door. 'What's changed?'

'Some went,' she said.

'I've read nothing about any trial,' I said.

She shrugged. 'They went, anyhow.'

'They must have been charged somewhere, for something,' I said.

She looked at me.

'But don't you understand, they were tools,' she said. 'We can't see why it's wrong to tunnel for uranium. It's valuable. Does it all belong to the Government, or something?'

'Uranium,' I said. I had forgotten that queer excuse. 'No, it doesn't.'

'Well, they said it was because of those men blown up in the tunnel,' she said. 'Manslaughter at least, they said.'

'Oh, that was it!' I said. I was surprised by that switch, for I had blown up the tunnel. But I could see what a splendid get-out it was for the State. Criminal negligence and all that. You could hold men for months mucking about with that kind of legal entanglement. I read newspapers as I walk over ground, fast, and have to look back to see where I've been.

Manslaughter and negligence had never occurred to me. I had been looking out for a disguised Official Secrets violation.

She put a hand on my knee. It sent the old urge running through me so that I knew my convalescence was over.

'Why have you come back?' she said.

'I left something behind,' I said.

'They'll kill you this time.'

'There might be a closer police watch now than there used to be,' I said.

'There is,' she said. 'But it won't make any difference. You know that. You must have known before you came. But that's you, isn't it? You just look for trouble.'

'No, I don't. I hate it, but it happens that what I have to find is nettled around with trouble. Like Hotspur.'

'Who's he?'

'His flowers were always in the nettles,' I said, and then being casual, 'There was no publicity, so no trippers came?'

'They sealed the place off, but then

it's so easy here. Nobody wants to come anyway. There's nothing here. Just Dead End.'

The Manor still empty?' I said.

She turned slowly, and there was a look in her face that made my heart hesitate.

'No,' she said.

The heart rushed on again like a dinner gong.

'What happened?'

'There was a will, it seems. This man has come to see what can be done.'

'What man?'

'A Chinaman. From Singapore,' she said.

'How in hell does that tie up with a derelict mansion in Wiltshire?'

She shrugged.

'It's to do with the will.'

'Whose will?'

She drank.

'Johnny's father,' she said.

An old clock struck midday from somewhere out in the back of the place.

I let it strike, then I said, 'It would have been Johnny's?'

'When he was twenty-one,' she said.

One comes up against all kinds of ironies. This one looked as if in killing Johnny to save myself I had dumped my fortune with him.

Magog, my fortune. Magog had been hidden in the Manor House. Magog had been the reason—and the only reason—I had come to Dead End in the first place. Now Johnny's rep had got there, a Chinese from Singapore.

'What's his name, honourable chink in the curtains?'

'Chang Lee,' she said. 'That's what it sounds like. I don't know for sure.'

'It's good enough. What kind of man is he?'

'Money rubs off him,' she said. 'That's all our lot want to know.'

'So when one door shuts another one opens?'

'It kept things going,' Laura said.

'When did he come?'

'Just September.'

'Anybody with him?'

'Yes. The people to see what can be done with it,' Laura said, and looked at me. 'Why do you worry so much?'

'I wanted to buy the place myself,' I said.

She put her head back and laughed.

'You damn liar!'

'Don't you believe anybody can make money out of Dead End?' I said. 'You listen to me, I can turn that place into a re-bore establishment for tired businessmen. I'm an expert in physical exercises for digestive ailments, nervous troubles—' (Well, so I am, because I belong to a gymnastic club, and I know that certain regular exercises under supervision take the pangs out of the two named and many others, and what's more, when the TBM aches from healthy exercise instead of the others he is Top Goon for the rest of the week.) 'I would have them here for a month course, gentle exercises, good food, everything of the best, but make 'em work it out, Laura. That's the secret. And I'd work it out of the old pendulous paunches, believe me. I'd make 'em feel good. There's room up there for everything I need, all the private rooms, the public rooms, a gym, a swimming pool—the lot.'

I got quite enthusiastic, though I had thought of this bust into the rich lands only that minute. For a moment I thought Magog might take second place in the Easy Money list, but then I had a head like that: it jumps at rainbow illusions like a trout.

She laughed heartily now.

'You think such a lot of rubbish, I don't know,' she said. 'What rich man would come here for a month?'

'He'd come here for a year if he thought he'd walk out young again,' I said. 'It's a best seller, youth. You only want it when you've had it. Let's have another drink, Laura. I must think what to do now.'

She got up, then stopped, facing the

door. I looked past her hour-glass silhouette. There were four men standing by the
broken corner of the fence across the yard,
staring at the pub door.

Their silence and the slow-chewing
attitude of watchfulness brought back
my first scared feelings of being alone
in Dead End.

This time I couldn't make any mistake
about what they meant. I had been
prepared in some measure, for some
of this, but then, I hadn't expected to
stay long.

I didn't know that a Chinese from
Singapore had taken up the seat in the
house of my fortune.

3

Laura hesitated in going back behind the
counter, her eyes on the men out there.
Then I saw her back stiffen defiantly and
she went on to get the drinks.

'It'll be hard this time,' she said, as she busied herself.

'It was hard last time,' I said.

'Not like this,' she said. 'Before they didn't want you in. Now they owe you something. You took away everything they dreamed about, killed some of their men and put a lot more away.'

'It's a bad score,' I said. I had tried not to put it quite so plainly to myself. It was depressing. 'Tell me about Chang Lee.'

'He's a big grinning yellow turnip,' she said. 'His head is round like a turnip. At the back you can see his hair grows out like the petals of a daisy. He cuts it like a little boy, with a fringe in front. He weighs as much as an ox but he dances on his toes like a fairy. He has a sense of humour. You'll like him.' She came round the counter again with the drinks. 'But don't trust him.'

'Who did he bring with him?'

'Two men and a girl secretary.' She put the glasses down and went to the door, hands on her hips. She reminded me of her daughter Linda, standing there like that. 'Anything you want, you layabouts?''

There was a grunt, then a laugh and a shuffle of boots on the dusty ground.

'Not yet!' a man called out.

I heard them laughing as they went away from the pub door. They left a queer silence. She turned and looked at me as if she felt the strangeness, too.

'Tell me about the two men and the girl,' I said.

'I know nothing of them,' she said. 'They don't talk to anybody. They don't smile. Like at a funeral when everybody is stiff and grim till the coffin's gone, then they laugh and get drunk. Well, these don't laugh and get drunk.'

'You don't see them often?'

'You don't see them often,' she agreed and laughed.

'But they're always there, somewhere behind him. You can bet on that.'

'They brought some furniture up there?

The place was bare, I remember.'

'There was a flat furnished right at the top,' she said.

'Johnny did it. The man said it was awful.'

'What man—Chang?'

'No, the other man.'

'Alaski?'

She shrugged and looked away. Alaski had been the big political shot in charge of the original Sin of Dead End. He had vanished completely. I had read about his vanishment; at least, odd published queries as to what had happened to him. He was of foreign extraction, naturalised, and the GB Public was ready to believe anything of such; even that they could go up in smoke.

The Affair at Dead End was closed. The assorted police had closed it after me. There was nothing of it left but Alaski, and he was as good as dead, for if he showed again he would be catching his head in a revolving door with all the police pushing in by the following three compartments.

It was assumed he had got away and would turn up, if he ever was seen to turn up, in South America. I had met him only once on a doorstep by moonlight.

Alaski would have gone from my grasshopper brain if it hadn't been for a long, black 600 Mercedes that came rustling by on the dusty road outside and went, leaving dust whorls behind, up to the road out.

'Who's that?' I asked. 'Chang?'

She nodded.

'There were four people in it,' I said casually. 'So there's nobody up at the Manor now?'

'I don't know,' she said. 'I wouldn't be sure of anything with that little lot. You can't trust foreigners.'

The big car went on up the winding pass and vanished behind the slopes.

'I could go up and see,' I said.

She looked at me steadily awhile.

'You're a damn fool,' she said. 'One

day you'll push your luck right over the edge.'

'Luck needs a push,' I said. 'Otherwise it doesn't come up often enough.'

I finished my beer. It was good. I would have liked some more, but I got up instead.

'Suppose I put up here?' I said. 'Formally this time.'

She laughed.

'It's all right with me,' she said. 'We have had to be pretty formal since the police stirred everything up. They come in every night now, look round, go out.'

'If they'd done it before it would have saved a lot of bother,' I said.

'Don't worry,' she said ironically. 'They come to see if anybody turns up. People they're looking for. Some got away, you know.'

I did not feel too easy about that, either. Magog was no formality. My business with Magog was definitely beyond the fringe of police approval. But then there are few ways you can pick up a fortune and official congratulations both together.

It was beginning to look like a bum welcome back, what with Chang up at the Manor and the police dropping in like warders at the cell peephole. That was leaving out the gentry hanging around outside to remind me of my past.

I'd expected some of the last, but the other two were surprises. Chang from Singapore or points east of nowhere was a real trick drop in the lap and it hurt. The police I might smooth round because I know them.

Then came another clanger, right in my ear.

'What happened to your girl-friend?' Laura said.

There was a kind of arsenic-treacle in her tone, a specially prepared mixture.

'Linda, you mean?' I said, side stepping.

'No, Jane,' said Laura.

'I have so many,' I apologised.

'Jane,' she repeated, showing her teeth.

'Oh yes, I remember,' I said. 'She sends her regards.'

'She told me she'd love you or shoot you, either way.'

'Janey told you that?' I said, my pulse knocking.

'When?'

'Not long ago,' said Laura.

I felt my face freezing, and when I put on a careless smile the skin tried to crack.

'She was here?' I said.

'She looked in,' said Laura.

'Looked in?' I said. 'Didn't she stay?'

'She just came. She said you were still in hospital, but you'd be down as soon as you were out.'

'So you expected me,' I said.

'I always expected you, without her,' said Laura.

'I take that both ways,' I said, trying to brighten up.

'Did she go up to the House?'

'I don't know,' Laura said. 'I don't have

so much time these days, with Linda gone, and having to keep a good front for the police.'

'You have a good front for anybody, Laura,' I said. 'But why didn't you tell me about Janey before?'

'She said to tell you when you were going up to The House.'

Dear Janey. She could read me like she reads the last page of a book. She always troubles me. Whenever I'm not with her I try to find every excuse for losing her, but when we touch again it's all gone and through the hoop I go and fall into a clown's bath full of whitewash.

'It was a kind of a greeting,' I said. 'What did she say?'

'The message?' Laura laughed. 'She just said she'd be waiting.'

'Well, there's nothing like a dependable girl-friend, Laura,' I said.

'Specially if you can depend on her to shoot you,' said Laura, innocently.

I looked round at the doorway, casually.

You never know with these women. They laugh when they've got you fixed in a trap, and I was in such a state of uneasy expectation that I even thought Janey might be standing in the door behind me.

'What else did she tell you?' I asked, acting as if I meant to go anyway.

'She just said that,' said Laura.

'I'll be back,' I said.

In the car I sat there a few seconds and thought of this situation. Janey was my partner when we first tried to get Magog. That we were tricked is beside the point, but she was as deep in that business as I was. She was a character girl with a character like hot steel. She was hot and she didn't give way on anything except by way of enjoyable resilience. She meant to win over the Magog business just as much as I did. She hadn't mentioned it lately when I'd seen her. She certainly hadn't mentioned she'd been to Dead End again.

That she had come here meant one thing only; she had meant to retrieve Magog without telling me, but she had gone away with her hands open.

Like me, she had found Chang in the way. But Janey did not stop at Changs—unless Chang was something very special indeed. Something she'd sooner leave me to deal with than try on her own.

If that was the truth, I was up against something more unpleasant than anything I'd thought of up to then. Janey wouldn't have let Magog alone for anything short of a sabre toothed tiger. There I glimpsed a likeness, for the sabre toothed tiger had had willy-nilly a kind of grisly grin, and Chang, Laura said, was a constant grin.

My suspicious nature, my fearful little soul clicked Chang into a Danger file at the start. It was lucky this did happen for I started off wary of him whereas, but for Janey, I needn't have thought him anything but some kind of agent from Singapore.

I started the engine. Laura suddenly appeared at the window.

'Don't push it too far,' she said, keeping her voice low and very urgent.

I looked past her to a couple of men lounging, looking at us.

'I'll be all right, Laura,' I said. 'You remember me.'

'It was all luck, last time,' she said. 'Nobody knew you. It's different now. Don't push it.'

She kissed her finger and tapped it on my nose. I felt an upsurge of heat and pleasure. I liked Laura. I like women. They do things for me.

It was a bumpy road. When the quarry had been working they had tarmacked the surface. It had broken, they had patched it and then the quarry had stopped working and now there were only the patches left, like bruises standing clear of the dust. It was like the rest of the place, built for a local prosperity which had died and left them nothing.

Come to think, it could almost bear a recuperation centre for the money makers. I could see the initial impulse; 'Get rid of that diet, friend, it can do nothing for you but take off shape where you don't want to lose it, make the stretched skin sag like crinkle bandages and bring you headaches and lack of faith in life: Be like the sabre toothed cat and eat what you like but learn how to work it off' and so on. I could begin to see the whole thing shaping up.

Which shows what kind of mind I have, that it can shy off a definite unpleasantness, and build up, colour up, sound up some stupid idea that only just came into my head as an excuse.

The alarm sounded above my dreams when my eyes flicked to the mirror and caught that Land-Rover steaming up behind and turning out so fast it reeled on its big tough wheels, beating the dust of Hell out of the road as it went.

In the flash of the moment of fear I knew he couldn't have just seen me, for you can see a long way along the road in Dead End. He must have been trying to come up on my blind spot.

Thinking on the lines of sabred toothed tigers I got the slinky notion in my mind of being eaten up by a Land-Rover, nursery type.

In fact it didn't do that. It came at me on the starboard quarter, big and high like a shouldering bully, and when it hit my front wing it shook through the car and jolted my shoulder in just the same way.

There wasn't a question of holding it. I was just shoved thirty degrees round from the forward motion with a kind of scream from underneath that I could hear even as my metal folded in front of me.

I did not remember the great gash by the side of the road where there had once been a protective fence, warning the wayward off. Only a few rotten posts remained and I smashed them down like noisy ninepins.

I went over the edge and suddenly I was driving down a sheer cliff, straight at

35

the ground of rocks and scattered bushes. There was a moment when I wished I had fastened my safety belt, then a moment I didn't as I threw myself along the seat and tried not to be thrown up through the roof.

Then all moments stopped.

CHAPTER II

I

It seemed whole minutes that the car rumbled, tore and shook over the rough slope down to the bottom of the crater. I wished I had watched my rear mirror, but I hadn't thought of other traffic in Dead End. By throwing myself along the seat I saved myself everything but the final bump which shook me from end to end and thudded the breath out of my body.

I switched off, just in case of fire, and lay still. Nothing happened for a long while, and then I heard boots scrambling down the slope behind the car.

My breath came back, and I breathed easily to soothe the nerves and ready the muscles, for I had the idea that the man coming down was not doing it to apologise.

I saw him stop by the side of the car and peer in. I kept still. What he thought, I don't know, but he muttered something and pulled the door open. I shot out my feet and got him right where it hurt him most. He doubled up, staggered and tumbled over on the dusty ground.

There was nobody at the top of the slope when I got out, but the front of the Land-Rover stood there, staring skywards. I went to the man and put my foot on the small of his back as he half rolled on the ground. He twisted his head against the earth. I had never seen him before. His face was not one I remembered from my earlier call at Dead End.

He was dark, olive skinned, and looked Spanish. I turned him over with my foot and kept a hand bunched in the pocket of my slacks.

'What's it about?' I said.

He looked up, frowning with pain and anxiety.

'What's it about?' I repeated and moved my hand so that he could see the bulge pointing down at him.

'Skid,' he said.

'Who told you to skid into me?'

He didn't like that. It seemed to take him by surprise, or perhaps it shook him when I was standing over him with what he now thought was a gun in my pocket.

'I was too fast,' he said quickly. 'It slid away with me.'

Where I stood I had only to lift my eyes to see the top of the bank by the truck. His eyes kept drifting the same way, as if expecting somebody. I didn't think there had been somebody with him in the wagon, or they would have spoken and I would have heard them in the bright stillness, but the house was close by and anyone could have seen the smash.

Perhaps somebody had been waiting to see it.

My stance was light and ready, so that I could make the cover of the car should anyone try to take me by surprise. But no one appeared over the edge.

I looked all round then, but there were only birds to be heard singing away in the trees clustered round the house. The man sat up, regarding me with dark eyes and a kind of sneer on his mouth.

'Where's everybody?' I said.

The man on the ridge caught my eye and I looked up there by the truck. He was like a human top, a huge body of great fatness, yet dwindling down to his feet as if he could spin on them. His face was fat and smooth and brownish yellow, and he looked down at me with what you might call a happy grin.

'Anyone hurt down there, please?' he said. He had that high, seesaw voice from the East, yet it sounded too thin and childlike to fit that gross body. It was as if some child spoke from behind him.

'Nobody yet,' I said.

The grin broadened slightly.

'Come up, then, please. It cannot be nice down there.'

'I'm worried about my car.'

'Ferdi will wind it up on the winch,' Chang said, and pointed to the Land-Rover.

'Get cracking, Ferdi,' I said, and grinned at the man as he got up from the dusty ground.

I let him go up the rocky slope ahead of me. Small stones and tiny dust avalanches followed his scrambling feet. He was still shaken, but I wasn't sure whether it was because of my rough treatment or a fear of this yellow man on the top of the bowl. There was certainly something about the benign grin which had a cold touch. You could imagine an ancestor of his with a ringside seat at a torture grinning just so. Or perhaps my imagination was jumping.

Ferdi went to the truck when he got to the top. I stood and dusted myself down with my hands.

'I am sorry you have such a welcome,' said Chang.

'I am sorry, too,' I said. 'It gives a bad impression.'

'There was a skid, perhaps?'

'There was a deliberate side-swipe and Ferdi bumped me down that rabbit hole,' I said.

'Oh, perhaps not!' said Chang, smiling more broadly. 'It would look like that because you are angry. Welcome to my house and we will calm you.'

'Your house?' I said.

I was going to rough this smooth spinning top up if I could, but I realised it would take some doing, and if I did finally do it, he would probably lose his temper and do me another way. It's funny how you tell yourself you must not do something because it will be bad for you, yet you do it all the same, as if you can't help badding yourself. Or perhaps it's a vague desire to see if you're right.

'My house for the time now,' he said, beaming again.

We began to walk towards the dark entrance gates and the old, peeling lodge, and it reminded me of Janey. We had made love in that lodge once, when it had seemed it might be the last time we would ever make anything.

'I come for a client,' Chang went on. His currant eyes slid in their slots towards me. 'But you will know of that, too, perhaps.'

'I have heard talk in the village,' I said. 'But I am here because I understand the place might be for sale.'

He showed a glimmer of surprise.

'Is that it?' he said. 'I did not know.'

'But isn't your client dead?' I asked.

'Alas,' he said, and crossed his hands on his fat chest, bending his head slightly.

'Then it must be for sale,' I said. 'Or is it sold already?'

'We are looking into the possibilities, I believe you say,' he said, walking on and dropping his hands.

'Then surely this is the time to consider an offer,' I said.

He shoved his hands into the pockets of his loose beige coloured jacket, and nodded his head as if in thought. Ahead of us on the overgrown drive a grey squirrel streaked gracefully across towards a tree on the left hand side.

Chang's hand came out of his pocket so quickly that the whole act took me entirely by surprise. I stopped in my tracks.

He came out with a tiny two-two pistol and shot the squirrel dead at the foot of the tree. As a practised revolver shot myself, often contesting the best shots in the police force, I can say I never saw a shot like that before. At fifteen feet, snap shooting a target as big as a squirrel you have to have an eye like a homing nose on an air-to-air missile.

'That was a shot,' I said.

'The grey squirrel is a pest,' Chang said, pocketing the little gun. 'Tree rats. But they are good targets for practice.'

'Where did you practise in Singapore?'

His eyes slid on to me again.

'Up country. In the jungle,' he said and beamed again. 'Why did you wish to buy?'

'I'm a developer,' I said. 'Jonathan Blake.' I gave him a card. They are good cards. They have nothing on them but 'Jonathan Blake.'

He looked at it intently, as if it said a good deal more. He drew his thumb across to test the engraving.

'They can imitate now,' I said. 'Just bruise it out. Ordinary print.'

'I was thinking perhaps I have heard of you before,' he said, smiling again.

'I try to get known,' I said, easily. 'That's my business.'

I think I detected a faint light of puzzlement in his black eyes, a kind of gleam. Such was understandable if he had heard of me before as some kind of secret agent who had come into Dead End masked as a traveller.

The inscrutability of Orientals seemed to be melting before my sharp eye, until I began to wonder why he behaved like this.

It would be quite simple for him to do me in at any moment. He had already tried the Land-Rover incident and made it look like an accident. But why, if he was secure here? Why should he pretend?

Could the daily police visit be treated with so much respect that Dead End had ceased to rule itself?

'You were here before,' he said.

It was impossible to tell from the tone whether it was a question or a soft statement.

'I was here before,' I said. 'That was when I thought this house had possibilities. On the side,' I added, 'I sometimes act as representative for firms needing a brief call in duff areas where their busy men don't go. It all adds to the pay.'

'One should take every opportunity,' said Chang, smoothly. 'It is the only philosophy.'

We came to the great door and the broad shallow stone steps rising to it. He turned there and made a welcoming gesture with his hand. It seemed so genuine I began to doubt my suspicions of him.

After all, why shouldn't he be straight? That truck-bashing trick might have been inspired by someone who remembered the dead and gone Johnny.

One of my weaknesses is the way I always tend to believe things are not so bad as they seem. Sometimes, of course, it turns out right, and often it turns out to be just an excuse.

We went up and into the house, the same bare, neglected empty house I had known before. It gave me the same chill in the stomach and almost stopped me from being optimistic.

But all the time I had been coming here I had borne in mind my insurance policy, which I had hidden back in the days of plenty. In my last visit there had been guns all over the place, and in the course of the expedition I had got me a .38—no matter how—and stacked it away in a hole in the garden wall, meaning it to be a safeguard for that time. It so happened I hadn't been able to get back to it, but I felt sure nobody else had.

The feeling that that gun was there buoyed me up. It was better than bringing one, for in suspicious circumstances people like Chang search cars and people.

As Chang ushered me towards the old staircase I saw a man standing in the doorway of an empty room on my right. He just stood there, watching. I looked at him and said good morning. He just went on standing there watching me. He looked like an Arab, dressed in Savile Row clothes. I shrugged my shoulders at him.

'Ali is taciturn,' Chang said, beaming by my side.

'You have an international stable,' I said as we mounted the stairs.

'One learns much more,' said Chang.

As I glanced back down the stairs and

in at the door, I saw Ali was balancing a knife on his palm, just as an expert knife thrower does.

It began to seem that Chang was putting on a show for me, designed to bring on palpitations. He might have been right, for despite his smile of welcome—maybe because of it—I began to feel some kind of gate was dropping behind me, like a portcullis.

The chill smell of the place, as if it hadn't warmed up with the day yet, began to be fringed with a scent. It was faint at first, then grew in richness as we went up.

'You live here for the time being?' I asked.

'For now only,' said Chang.

'I understood the place was empty.'

'There are quarters to live,' said Chang.

The quarters to live were in fact the whole top floor of about twenty rooms which once had housed the staff, in the days of staff.

At the top of the stairs there was a length of carpet running along a passage. There were doors on one side of the passage, facing windows on the other. The woodwork had been painted in parts, as if someone had got tired of it. Or because Johnny had died in the middle of it.

I didn't like the way I kept remembering Johnny like that. It was like a ghost following along behind me.

The scent at the top floor was strong, almost sickly in its intensity. A woman was standing at one of the doors, and as I saw her I felt myself hesitate inside.

She might have been Chinese. I don't know, but she was Oriental and so smoothly beautiful she was like the girls the man painted in green and still made them look sexpots. She was tall and wore a black silk dress that hugged her all the way. It could have been painted on, and seemed at the time more devastating than if she had had nothing on at all.

'This is my wife,' said Chang.

The woman bowed her head slowly, almost in mockery, her eyes not leaving mine till the last moment of her tilting. Chang snapped his fingers. The woman turned and went into the room.

I was disappointed to see that she was not there when I went in ahead of Chang. There was another door she must have gone through.

The room was furnished by Johnny. There was too much of everything, and everything was too much.

Chang shut the door.

'Now, Mr. Blake," he said, smiling still, 'why are you so eager to die?'

He caught me with one foot off the ground, but I got it back without too much of a pause.

'Oh, but I'm not,' I said. 'In fact, the opposite. My object in buying this house is to make a living.'

He laughed and his fat belly shook.

'You will have a drink,' he said, turning to a table. 'It will not be poisoned.'

I didn't think it would be, somehow, for the odd idea came into my head that Chang wanted to know something before I was finalised.

He gave me Scotch. I know Scotch and it was all right, and did me good. Until then I hadn't realised how dry I was with nerves and tension.

'You have come alone?' Chang asked.

'I don't want to let anyone in on it,' I said. 'There are too many developers chasing each other. You get an idea, then they all get it.'

'Tell me your idea,' he said smoothly, and drank some Scotch as if to show it was pure.

'You won't sell it?'

His belly shook again as he laughed.

'That is not my business,' he said.

So after a timely hesitation, I told him my crackpot scheme for a rich man's health resort, and he watched me all the time. I knew I was putting on a good, frank open face for that's one thing I can put on. In fact, I half believed the rigmarole myself.

When I had finished he seemed to be considering it.

'Let us go round and see where you would arrange all this,' he said, moving quickly towards the door.

So we made a long, detailed tour of the chill, empty place and I thrashed some life into the grey dusty cells by painting them up with my imagination. In the ballroom, we stopped. It was as big as a theatre.

'This would be the gymnasium,' I said.

He nodded, his eyes sliding from side to side in their slots as if checking my ideas for the vast room.

This tour was puzzling me, for I knew very well he was up to something, yet I couldn't see what. Touring the house seemed on the face a waste of time, and yet I was sure there was something behind it, something unpleasant for me.

Now and again as we went around I saw somebody coming in or going out of a doorway, Ali, another man I couldn't recognise and once Ferdi, who must by then have winched my car up out of the pit. I didn't mention this then. I left it for an excuse to get out later—if this well-mannered charade was to continue, I mean.

The tour of the ground floor ended. We saw the cellars and then came up to the first floor. Chang did not show any quickening of interest, but I felt one. I felt it hammer in my chest as we went along, entering room after room, slowly approaching the one where Magog was hidden.

Then I guessed this might be the reason for the tour. He was deliberately taking me round, room by room, in order to try and cheek my reaction at each one. As if he was some kind of human lie detector.

Well, he had a good patient in me, I reckoned. The idea that he was watching me for reactions made my feelings tighter, my hammering so intense I had the idea he could hear it. But he padded on at my side, a flesh mountain, nodding to my fatuous ideas.

We came to Magog's room. He gestured to me to go in, just as he had done to the other rooms, yet this pose now seemed to have a sinister meaning.

I went in, the beating in my ears very strong, so that I did not hear his soft movements behind me.

The first shock came when I saw that the room was not empty. It was furnished as a kind of bed-sitter, but with a desk by the window and a tatty, frayed-out Wilton on the floor. I noticed it because it had frayed so badly that you could catch a foot in it if you were not being careful.

'Ferdi uses this room,' said Chang.

'Just this one?' I said, grinning to hide my uneasiness. 'Doesn't he feel lonely down here all by himself?'

Chang laughed again.

'This is the only room that looks right down the road,' said Chang pointing to the window. 'That is why he chose it. He likes to look down the road. He used to drive Ferraris, but his nerve went and he has fits of violence very difficult to control. I have had much trouble with him.'

Chang looked as if he had enjoyed the trouble he had had with Ferdi.

'What does he do?' I asked, not anxious to leave the room.

This room was where Magog was hidden. Janey had found that out, but she had not found Magog. Nor had I any more idea of where it was hidden. For me it was going to mean stripping the place to the brick walls, and maybe even deeper in than that.

Such an exercise was going to be difficult, but with Ferdi hanging about being temperamental it was going to be almost impossible.

I had the treacherous feeling I ought to chuck in then. I didn't stand much chance, but I might get out if I just stuck to my health home and let Chang see me off.

'Ferdi?' said Chang, watching me with his slits. 'He goes berserk with people.

Suddenly he imagines they are coming up behind him. That was how he finished racing his motor cars. He got the idea somebody was coming up behind him and so he went faster and faster and faster until he could not hold it any more and he crashed. When he recovered he was not normal, and when he killed the man for nothing it was very difficult for me to get him out of the country.'

'Oh, he killed somebody?' I said, interested.

'Tore him to pieces,' said Chang evenly. 'Just for nothing. He did not even know the man.'

'How very impulsive,' I said, looking round the room.

Ferdi's reading matter seemed to be confined to horror comics of which there were three piles, all dog-eared and well-read. There were no signs that he smoked.

'When he has no work to do, he stays here all day, pacing up and down and up and down, like a tiger,' said Chang. 'It will drive the others mad, now and again, but they dare not object for he might—lose his temper. They know what happened before, you see.'

Chang was determined to impress upon me the unpredictable ferocity of Ferdi. In the first place, he knew that Ferdi would not like me, and to multiply a normal dislike by all this talk of tigerish fury was a deliberate attempt to demoralise.

'This is the only room that looks out?' I said. 'I hadn't noticed.'

'The trees grow all around,' Chang said, beaming. 'Only this window looks in the right direction, between breaks in the trees.'

Which could have been why it was chosen for Magog's interment.

Chang sat on the edge of the desk.

'Perhaps you would like longer to consider?' he said.

I smelt trouble in the question, perhaps because I was guilty about the room. I should have realised that there had been no other room where he could have rested a moment to talk, for they had all been empty.

'I thought it was you considering,' I said.

He shook his head.

'I would have to have a complete plan to offer,' he said. 'The trustees, you understand, must be satisfied that yours would be the best for the estate.'

This sudden twist was somewhat unsettling. I felt the bottom falling out of my open faced pretence of a plan, for I hadn't expected his twist to he considering it. I hadn't thought of it.

'Do not hurry, please, Mr. Jonathan Blake,' he said, raising a hand. 'You will stay with us a day, perhaps, and work out your details with us.'

I was delighted and frightened all at once. I didn't want to be snapped into the trap of this house, but on the other hand, I would be close to Magog, even though Ferdi did sleep with it.

'I have booked a room at the inn,' I said. 'There's no reason to cancel that. I could walk to and fro.'

The odd humour of the situation appealed to me. Walking to and fro a tiger's den you intend to burgle all under the guise of putting up a business proposal was rich indeed. The fact that Chang suspected me as much as I did him made it richer.

'That is as you wish,' he said. 'You could do your work here.'

'Why not here?' I said. 'There's a desk.'

Chang laughed.

'Ferdi wouldn't like that,' he said. 'He has a little thing about a desk. He wanted one to put his feet on. He is rather like a child now.'

'Except when he goes rough.'

'Yes, indeed. That can be very disturbing.'

'All right,' I said. 'I'll sell you if it's the last thing I do. I want the place, but it'll take a day or two working up a specification.'

'There is no hurry,' said Chang, and bowed his head.

2

It was incredible, but it had happened. Or perhaps I was being smoothly drawn into an Oriental conception of a trap which was not obvious to me?

He gave me a room on the top floor. It looked out at elm tree tops, and a short slate slope down to a lead gutter behind a parapet. When I shoved my head out of the window I saw a regiment of dormers drawn up on either side of me.

The room was furnished with a strange conception of an office. It had a polished table, a working chair, a couple of deep leather armchairs, a filing cabinet and a long couch, I imagine, to relax on after my tearing brain-work. There might have been no difficulty in digging up such a hodge-podge because Johnny had been himself a collector of anything whose shape he fancied no matter what its use had been.

By the time this was arranged, we had lunch, a chow dished up by Madame whose delights kept drawing my eyes all the meal. Chang ignored her all the time, and she seemed meekly tuned in to this contempt and hardly said a word all through.

There was a fourth with us, the secretary. The secretary it had been who had ordered the collection of furniture. She was a blonde of around thirty, big and with a mannish air sometimes, though I got the drift in my head that, in the sight of God, as they say, she was Mrs. Chang One in order of choice. I don't know why I thought that, but when I did Mrs. Chang's meekness seemed suddenly poignant and sad; a strange emotion for me to feel over such a beauty.

The secretary was a Greek and was called Lucia, or something near that. She spent a good deal of the time staring at me with cold blue eyes, sizing me up, judging me like a prize ox.

'You are a big man,' she said. 'Do you fight?'

'Not if I can avoid it,' I said.

'But you are very athletic,' she persisted.

'I am interested in the art,' I said.

'They were born in Greece,' she said. 'On Olympus.'

I had the feeling that if I said people ran around before that there would be a row. The feeling of talking to her was that of walking between two high roofs on a telephone line.

Chang had certainly got himself a crew that made one feel uneasy. What with Ferdi the explosive, Ali who gloomed around the place sharpening and balancing knives, and Lucia who seemed determined to challenge all the way in the hope of finding a weakness, there was going to be no peace in this house.

It was even going to be difficult to find quiet enough to get round to Ferdi's room.

And I had to do that, no matter what.

She kept digging, fair Lucia. She deliberately tried to rouse me, make me angry. That isn't difficult usually, but I had my neck to lose and for once I steered a cautious track.

Chang did not seem to take notice of what we said, but I knew he judged every word. He gave one the horrid feeling that everything a person did was taken into account, the smallest action, the tiniest slip or error, all were stored for use within this Chinese computer.

That was the second time I had compared Chang to some electronic machine. As I realised it I felt I was perhaps not so far wrong.

The afternoon was hot. Even the house had warmed to the sun by then. I went to my office, closed the door and listened for a while.

Outside Chang and Lucia spoke a few words I did not catch, then parted, one going lightly downstairs. Lucia, I thought.

After that there was a silence.

The silence was broken by a muttering that seemed to be coming from my room. It was a strange sound, fading, then growing loud and sharp, then dying again.

I tracked it to the fireplace, and thought of birds in the chimney. But birds usually get into chimneys for one reason, to make a nest, and this was no time of year for making nests.

I listened again. It was a man talking, but the flue was distorting the voice so that it whispered hollowly, and I could not make out any words. Now and again the voice became violent, then died once more.

'Then I realised why I couldn't understand any words. The man was talking Spanish. I could make out the vowel sounds and some word endings and once I spent a week in the Costa Brava for a girl who didn't turn up, so I learnt a little Spanish from another girl. But understanding that sweetie was different

65

from trying to decipher this lot, distorted by the flue.

It was Ferdi. Ferdi was pacing, as Chang had said he did, up and down the room. That accounted for the voice getting loud and then fading, then getting loud again. It was Ferdi, talking to himself, for there was no answering voice.

Old chimneys are sometimes built running one into the other on top of each other going upwards. Which meant that Ferdi's room was directly underneath my office.

My excitement at the discovery was tempered by a brief wonder as to whether this had been arranged, but I couldn't see why it should be.

Chang and Company couldn't know Magog was there, or they'd have stripped the place long ago.

Also I felt they wouldn't still he here if they had found it.

Magog was worth enough to satisfy even Chang and his large staff of freaks.

I knelt at the fireplace listening, but before I could make any sense, the ranting stopped. Ferdi had perhaps gone to his horror comics for solace.

The chimney was old. Peering up under the fire hood I saw a big square patch of sky. It was the old type of chimney that boys had been sent up.

But as Lucia said, I am a big man. I feared getting myself jammed in the flue in an attempt to get down to Ferdi's room, and broke out in a sudden sweat of claustrophobia.

I got up, either because of that or because instinctively I knew someone was going to come into the room. There were two doors, one into the passage and one into the room next door.

It was the second which drew my attention. I went to the couch, got on to it and lay there, taking a notebook and ballpoint from the desk as I went. Then I posed 'at work' and waited.

The door opened and she came in. I

just lay there, frozen, looking at her as she came in.

She wore just a plain pair of golden ear-rings.

CHAPTER III

1

It was quiet out in the passage. I stood on the carpet strip and looked up and down the corridor. The sun slanted in at the line of dormers at a high angle and dust whirled lazily. I envied it. It had nothing to do but dance because it wanted to. I had to dance because I didn't.

The silence was desperate. I wished somebody would come and see me, but there was no one.

The stairs were uncarpeted and I made a fair row going down them to the corridor below. No one was there either, but I knew Ferdi was in his room, for I had heard him muttering again when the naked beauty had come into my solitude.

As I came to the door of Magog's room, where Ferdi was spending his afternoon's soliloquy, I heard him at it again. I shoved the door open.

He was caught striding across the room. He turned back and almost snarled like an animal, his olive face growing darker with rage. His fists were clenched. He was all ready.

'Can't you make less noise down here?' I said. 'I can't work with this continual buzz.'

He just stood there, staring. Then his eyes lifted to the ceiling, and there was a puzzled look in them.

He knew about Madame Chang, then. No doubt they all knew about her. I began to feel I was right from the start, that she was my trap, and that her entry was no blind accident.

'I make no noise!' he said, and began to look very angry.

'You were shouting to yourself,' I said, determined to work him up and see what his temper was really like.

'It came up through the floor.'

He stepped towards me.

'You try to make me a fool, eh?' he shouted.

'Not necessary. Keep quiet and prove you aren't.'

'You are very clever, very sharp,' said Ferdi, and then he forgot that I was not supposed to be dead yet.

He snatched a knife from his belt and came for me.

I got to one side just in time and tripped him as I went. He was too worked up to be accurate, though he would have got me fairly had I stayed put.

He crashed into the door, which slammed and shook the stout wall of the place. The knife blade was driven right through the hefty panel, so that he fought but could not get it out.

As he struggled with it, I got him across the throat with the back of my forearm and a knee in his back spun him up and over in a backward somersault. It was better than anything I had done at the gym.

He crashed to the floor, and it shook everything.

The more noise the better for me. I wanted Chang or somebody to come in and find me playing around with Ferdi and not cavorting with Madame Chang.

Ferdi got up and went for my middle when he was still on his knees. I had expected him to get to his feet first and he got me prettily.

His grip round my waist almost broke my spine and I had to knee him three times before I got free. By that time I was hurt and angry, so I hit him as he got up and slung him backwards across the bed. He was resilient, for he twisted and came off the end of the bed and at me again.

It was then that the door opened and Chang appeared there with the secretary behind him.

'Stop, stop!' the secretary snapped out.

Ferdi stopped. Whatever his tigerish

temper was like in truth it seemed very quickly tamed in certain circumstances. He stood there panting, glaring at the door, his big hands swinging like an ape's.

'What has happened?' asked Chang urbanely.

'I couldn't work, he was kicking up such a row down here,' I said.

Chang's smile was utterly disbelieving, and he bent his head slightly to accept the lie. He raised his hand and signalled over his shoulder.

The secretary went away, and I guessed she went up the stairs to my room.

'I am sorry that there should have been this interference,' Chang said blandly. 'Perhaps Ferdi had better find something to do. Where is Mr. Blake's car?'

'By the dip,' said Ferdi sullenly. 'I winched him.'

'Bring it in,' said Chang. 'And see if there is damage. We are responsible.'

Ferdi looked as if he would refuse, and just stood there breathing very hard and slow and glaring at Chang. Suddenly he changed his mind, his shoulders slackened. He turned away, got a light jacket off the bed, slung it over his shoulder and went out.

Chang looked at me.

'Now you may continue, Mr. Blake, please.'

'Thank you,' I said. 'I'm a jumpy sort of a person. My thoughts are easily disturbed.'

'I am sure,' Chang beamed.

He watched me go up the passage and the stairs. I heard the door of Magog's room shut and then nothing. At my own door I hesitated, you bet, but I heard nothing inside.

When I opened the door, the room was empty.

2

I thought a lot then. The room below

would be empty for a while. On the other hand, I would have to produce something as the result of my afternoon's labours, and I am a very slow writer. Also I hate writing, which makes it slower. With me anything I hate doing is hard to get started, but when there is something else I would rather do as well, it's impossible.

A quick temporary solution struck me. I sketched the plan of the house roughly on sheets of paper. That would be a good start. After all, at first I would have to marshal the ideas and sketching was the way.

The sketches looked good, I thought, and scattered them liberally over the table.

Then I went to the door and listened. It was a wonderful household for silence. You hardly ever heard anything unless somebody spoke, which was usually from directly behind you. A creeping lot.

When I opened the door, nobody was in the corridor. I had the excuse that I would say I had dropped a ballpoint down in the room where we had fought, but no one appeared to make it to.

I went down once more to Magog's room.

This had once been one of the principal bedrooms, measuring about twenty feet square with a small dressing-room opening off it on the left.

When the door was firmly shut behind me I looked round the room, making a mental note of everything about its structure. The walls had been panelled in wood, painted over white. The fireplace was slightly Adamesque, also white, but a basket grate had been taken out and a lot of soot and red rust lay on the iron shoulders of the basket holder.

There were three tall windows, sashes, set in the deep walls, with shutters that folded back into the reveals on either side.

Only the third—the right hand window nearest the fire—looked out past the trees and down the road to the scatter of cottages round the pub which passed for the village.

The ceiling was heavily moulded with plaster all round the edges but plain in the middle. From there an electric wire hung down with a solitary bulb on it.

Cupboards were set in the panelling on either side of the fireplace, with brass ring handles. I opened these, but they were empty, with plastered backs and sides.

The skirting that ran round the room had shrunk with the years and in places did not meet the floorboards by as much as a half inch. The floorboards themselves had been often mended, and there were joints where there shouldn't have been and strips of the wood were lighter. Yet all these details I could see showing beyond the sea of tatty Wilton, seemed to have stayed unmoved for many years.

The dressing-room had three cupboards, plastered inside with shelves. One contained a lot of old left-over rolls of wallpaper and nothing else.

It looked as if Chang had just come in, thrown some furniture into Magog's room for Ferdi as a lookout guard and left it at that.

There was no sign anywhere that anyone had been looking for anything.

It is very difficult to stand in a room scattered with furniture and to try and see it bare and empty. Standing by the door I tried to do that, and to put myself in the position of someone seeing it thus and looking for a hiding place for Magog.

There would be floor, panelled walls, the fireplace, and the reveals of the window openings where the shutters folded in.

The cupboards were plastered inside, and were therefore out. What was left didn't seem much. It didn't seem enough.

Almost idly I went along the windows and unfolded the shutters and looked behind them. The backs were eased with wood, but I could see that the paint had not been disturbed for years.

The natural place to hide something

would be the inviting throat of the brick-lined fireplace, but it seemed too natural. The next natural place was under the floor, and without moving the desk and stripping up the worn-out carpet I couldn't really see if anything had been disturbed there.

The door opened suddenly. I hadn't heard anything, and it caught me bending to lift the edge of the carpet.

Lucia the secretary came in. I was slightly behind the desk and palmed my ballpoint in time.

'There it is,' I said, straightening. I showed her. 'We had a scuffle. It must have dropped out then.'

She closed the door behind her and looked at me. She was a very Nordic Greek, very fair hair and blue eyes and tall and with a rather grand bearing. She watched me through big framed spectacles that were so clear they seemed to have no lenses.

'He will be gone all afternoon,' she said

in her mid-Atlantic English. 'You have plenty of time.'

There was the beginning of a smile on her face.

'But I found it,' I said, clipping it into my hip pocket.

'The pen, yes. But what else were you looking for?'

'Nothing I know of,' I said.

'You have been in here—' she looked at her wrist watch, '—eleven and a half minutes to now.' She dropped her arm and watched me.

'I just couldn't find it,' I said. 'I'm in no hurry.'

I leaned against the desk and cocked my head at her.

'I have been finding out about you, Mr. Blake,' she said quietly. 'It has been very interesting.'

'I was born between two houses, my stars are all to hell and I get misunderstood over everything,' I said.

'But you make very strong efforts to—put

things right,' she said. 'I judge from what you did when you were here before.'

'When I was here before,' I said, 'I came as an innocent traveller, and I got pushed around, shoved, kicked and almost murdered. Now when you think I wasn't doing anything but trying to sell a few items, it isn't surprising I got cross about it.'

'Very cross,' she said and smiled again.

'What is this about?' I said. 'I should have thought in the circumstances you should have been referring to my financial standing.'

'Have you one?' It was sly, knowing.

'No property developer has one. He borrows them,' I said.

'You should know,' she said, 'that there would be people in this village who would want to kill you. Yet it was worth the risk of coming back.'

'I think I can make some money here,' I said. 'After all, the police drop in now. It's not so isolated as it was.'

She folded her arms.

'Tell me what you want,' she said. 'I would help you to get it.'

I was sure she didn't know about Magog, but she knew *something* was there. She knew I hadn't come for peanuts or gym schools, so that part of my game was open to her; just the detail was missing, which at this stage didn't make much difference as I was missing it, too.

But Lucia was top dog here. I was sure she could wheedle Chang when she wanted. She could fix me to have this room.

But if she did that, all the others would be gathered outside.

No, that wouldn't be any good.

It is always my tendency to jump at an opportunity even though there might be trouble behind it.

'I believe you want to discuss something,' I said.

As I watched her I knew that if I accepted her help, it would turn out to be trouble later, but if I didn't, it would mean trouble now.

I never seem to get any decent clean, clear straightforward problems to solve. There's always some muddy fringe round the ones I get.

'I want money,' she said. 'A lot.'

The answer surprised me. I just hadn't expected anything so brutal.

'But you don't believe I've got any,' I said.

'Not now. But we are talking of the future, are we not?'

Make no mistake, Magog could keep a lot of people in luxury for a long time. It represented more than one would reasonably require or even covet.

'We should agree,' she went on. 'It seems that your choice is very limited. Either you have my help, or you will be dead.'

'I do hate these bloody sentimental ways of putting things,' I said. 'In any case, one does not decide these things in a flash. I mean, I didn't expect anyone to be here when I came. It was such a surprise to find Chang and the rest all securely lodged.'

She leaned back against the door.

'As you said, there's no hurry,' she almost purred. 'You just go on as Chang rather expects you to, working on your plans for the house, and then, when you are ready, you let me know.' She turned to the door to go out.

'Supposing I want something?' I said.

She looked over her shoulder.

'Ask me,' she said, and then went out.

3

So far I had been roughed up only twice, in a car crash and in the room with Ferdi, but both had been Ferdi, and he was unpredictable. What I didn't like was the way the others just seemed quiet and confident, as if I were some kind of performing rabbit in a cage.

I was quite alone, and as such, stood little chance of getting away with it. But there was a weapon to my hand without the pistol hidden in the wall outside.

These babies were playing against each other. The house was divided. Not that that is always foolproof for the attacker; a turncoat can spin round a second time and be right back where he started, which can be behind you.

All the same, I felt Lucia was a strong weapon.

The fact that she knew there was something in this room I wanted was unpleasant, but she did know, and I couldn't alter that now.

I decided to get on and look, without touching anything, for I didn't want Ferdi to get the notion somebody had been digging around.

My further search didn't help, though I pulled the ragged carpet up in sections to look under. With the way the floor had been mended it was difficult to tell in some places whether any of the patchwork had been done recently or years ago.

The time was slipping on. I decided to go out and think about this room and try and get some kind of scientific way of searching it.

I went into the corridor and up the stairs. At the top, Mrs. Chang came gliding by, back in her skin tight silk dress, and the full impact of her hit me again. She hit me either way, dressed or undressed.

She smiled at me and went on by with a gracious bow of her head.

I knew she didn't remember a thing about coming into my room showing just her ear-rings.

Then she slowed and stopped, staring ahead. I watched as she turned slowly back to me, her hands clasped in front of her. I leant against the landing rail.

'Do you like it here?' I said.

'It is very beautiful,' she said. She came close and her voice was very soft as she said, 'It is not good for you. Go.'

'I can't,' I said as quietly. 'I've got work to do.'

'You will never finish it,' she said.

She turned and went away down the passage. I looked all round, then followed her. She turned in at a door and I was behind her. She stopped in the room and turned round to me.

'I don't understand,' I said. 'But tell me this, why have you come here?'

'It is work my husband has to do,' she said. She was quite expressionless.

'You came here straight from Singapore?'

'Yes.'

'But how did the message come to your husband? By a letter?'

'I do not know. He has an office.'

'But suddenly he said you must go to England?'

'Yes. It was after the man came. He stayed several days, and it was when he went that we had to come.'

Then abruptly the idea came.

'This man,' I said, 'he was tall and had a big nose like a beak and he wore an eyeglass or there were marks round his left eye where he puts the eyeglass in.'

At last her almond eyes came to life, whether from fear or surprise I did not know.

'Yes, he has the marks,' she said. 'And sometimes he goes to take the glass from his eye, but nothing is there. Then he is very cross and is frightened to be seen. But you know him?'

'Yes, I know him,' I said. 'It was here that I saw him last.'

Alaski had disappeared, but I was sure that the visitor in Singapore had been no less than the departed politician. It seemed to help, though at the time I couldn't see why. Alaski was leader of the plot in Dead End and had remained unsuspected until the very last few minutes.

If he had got Chang to come back on his behalf, what for?

The organisation at Dead End had been

smashed up. The authorities would not have left a tiny bit that could be used again. After all, it was no small thing these anarchists had been out to do and they had damned near done it. It was certain sure they wouldn't have been left a second chance.

Then what else had Alaski left in Dead End? Surely the original plot had been enough?

One thing was sure; had the motive been Magog, then Alaski would have known where it was, and he would have got it before he left. He wouldn't trust a gang of international roughs to get it for him.

I made up my mind then to go back to the inn.

'Will you tell your husband I have gone back?' I asked her. 'There are certain papers I wish to look up.'

'Of course.'

She bowed her head. She was dead inscrutable.

I went back to my room, piled the

sketches and then went out. There was nobody around at all. When I got out to the sun on the drive I looked round. Away to the left, by some stable buildings, Ferdi was hammering the front of my car. He had a grudge against it, by the look of him.

The overgrowth was almost jungle after the rich summer, and I wandered off in amongst the bushes. Sun-drenched leaves shimmered all round me. They hadn't even begun to thin.

At the crumbling wall I stopped and looked round again, though I was almost completely cased in with vegetation. Nobody could have got near me without a rustle.

I counted the rough stones along, then pulled some moss out from between the ones I had remembered. My fingers touched the haft of the gun and I pulled it out. Again I looked round, then slipped the heavy lump into my pocket.

The way along by the wall was easy. I

came out by the lodge and looked back. Ferdi could just be seen round the edge of a clump of bushes. I strolled up to him.

'No hurry,' I said. 'I don't expect to want it.'

He glowered at me. It was a dark brilliant fire in his eyes, a lunatic light. I thought he would clunk me one with the heavy rubber hammer in his hand, but he relaxed, nodded and went on donging the metal.

'I'll walk to the pub,' I said.

No harm in letting everybody know how open it all was. I went out and along the hot, dusty road towards the tumbledown hamlet. There were one or two men moving about in the fields. Another was leaning against the rear wheel of a rusted-up tractor, watching me. He didn't move except just to nod his head, as if something satisfied him.

Suddenly, I remembered him. It was Fred, the man who could scent like a dog.

It was surprising, because I had been

sure Fred had been in the gang when the mine shaft had blown up, but I must have been wrong. Recognising him made me uneasy, for I knew very well he would hate me with considerable force.

I am at heart a peaceable man, and not all that keen on being hated. It makes for tensions.

The inside of the pub was quiet, a few old flies doing circuits and bumps on the hanging brass oil lamp in the middle of the bar room.

'Laura!'

She came in a little while, up on the landing at the top of the stairs which led down into the bar.

'Come on up here,' she said, and turned her back while I came. 'You can have Johnny's room. It is the best one, really.'

I suspected a macabre sense of humour. It isn't pleasant to use the bed of a man you have shot dead, and to lie there and see all his peculiarities round about the room.

'You can lock it so nobody can get in,' she said, walking along the passage ahead of me. 'No other room is like that.'

I relaxed. Of course, that was true. Johnny's room was lined with door-knockers and rather odd erotic pictures and ornaments, but the door had three locks and there were bars on the windows.

'You're very thoughtful, Laura,' I said. 'I don't know why I deserve it.'

She turned at the end of the passage and faced me with her back against Johnny's door.

'You can do something for me, too,' she said.

'Mention it.'

'I have nothing but this old wreck of a place,' she said. 'I should have had something from Johnny. He had a great deal—not what his father left, but his own.'

'Well, what happened to it?' I said.

'I don't know. Nobody can find it, and there's nothing in writing.'

'Where would he have left it? Was it money?'

'Yes, there would have been money. He was very mean always, used to hoard, like the door-knockers.' She shrugged and watched me with a long, slow gaze.

I felt very pleased for this had led right into the channel I had meant to reach somehow. When I had been last here Laura had lived at the Manor House.

'Well, you've looked here, I suppose?'

'Yes.' She nodded. 'He probably left it at the Manor, somewhere. He used the house a lot.'

'You know something about it,' I said. 'Haven't you got any idea where he might have stacked his dough?'

Her eyes narrowed.

'There is a chapel,' she said.

'I know.'

'Once or twice I saw him coming out of there as if he didn't want to be seen. Nobody goes in there, you see. It has a big padlock and rusty old chains on the door. Superstitious people don't like places like that.'

'He wasn't particularly superstitious.'

'No, perhaps not, but I am.'

'Oh. You want me to have a look in there?'

'I don't know where else,' she said.

I looked into the box room by my left. It was open and empty save for old boxes. I looked up to the trap in the ceiling which led into the attics.

'What's the matter?' she said.

'Had an odd feeling somebody was nearby,' I said.

'There's nobody here,' she said, looking round in puzzlement.

'How would you know? The doors have been open all day.'

'I'm sure.'

I took her word for it.

'I'll help you look,' I said. 'You help me.'

'What do you want?'

'Did you ever see Alaski, the chief of

the old organisation?'

'He came now and again,' she said evasively.

'He—employed you?'

'He was the chief,' she said.

'Do you know how he got away?'

'It was a little while before the police came, so I heard,' she said. 'He could have got away easily.'

'Did he have any belongings up at the house?'

'He used to bring suitcases with his things and his work.'

'His work?'

'He was always working. Papers, papers all over the place. All night long making plans. He was never still. When I told him about it he used to laugh and say what you had to do was plan something completely, then put it into operation and plan another. Keep working, he used to say, and he did.'

'So that while he was here over the old operation he could have been working on something different?'

'Oh, he was!'

'Do you know what it was?'

'I don't know. There were a lot of plans and drawings and photographs and maps.'

'Couldn't it have been the old operation, maps of the mine workings and that kind of thing?'

'Oh no. All those were destroyed before. He didn't risk anything lying about, material evidence he called it. He said you could wriggle out of any evidence provided there was nothing in writing.'

'He was a sharpish specimen,' I said.

Again I had the instinctive feeling that somebody was there near us. I turned and looked back along the passage, then I went along it slowly to the end, where I looked down into the empty bar.

'What's the matter with you?' she said, almost angrily. 'You trust me, don't you?'

'Of course, Laura,' I said. 'It's just that I

don't think you can be sure there's nobody here with us.'

'Who would it be, then?'

'There are lots of people it could be, Laura,' I said. 'Strange as it may seem to look at me, I'm a kind of jampot and there are a lot of wasps here.'

'You don't think that I would trick you?' She looked very dark, angry, demanding an answer.

'Not if you want my help,' I said, going back down the passage.

'Why, you—' She came up behind, spitting in rage.

'Where did you put my bag?' I said.

'In the room. Johnny's room.'

Instead of opening Johnny's door I went into the box room and gazed up at the attic. She watched, breathing hard. I grabbed the ladder and climbed up it to the long, ship-like extent of the attics, with all their stacks of rubbish and brass knobs, old picture frames and things.

There were a hundred places where

anybody could hide. I knew. I had hidden there myself. Something ticked irregularly, something loose being tickled by a light breeze from outside.

I went along, very quietly, looking into every bay, peering in the shadows behind the great sloping roof beams.

The water in the big tank slopped faintly, but that was all.

I was certain nobody was up there, but still I couldn't shake off that odd warning sense that somebody was watching, waiting for me.

I made no sound as I went back to the trapdoor and stopped a little way from it, so that I could just see slantingly down through the opening and get a fairly shallow angle on the door of Johnny's room.

Laura was looking up at the trap, but she did not see me. I had stopped just in time. She looked down again, moving quickly and almost in a panic.

She threw the door of the strange room

open, and I could see into it, the rich pieces of rug scattered on the floor, some of the brass door-knockers on the far wall, a picture of fruit which on close inspection turned out to be nudes. I saw these, things that I remembered.

I also saw a good deal of the rich, brass bed, and a man lying on it, still and quiet. She was looking at him as if to make sure he was still there.

My heart stopped absolutely and I felt suddenly sick with horror.

The man on the bed was Johnny.

CHAPTER IV

I

I just stood there looking down through the slot at the unbelievable. Everything seemed to be still for a few awful seconds, and then it burst.

Laura let out a wild scream. Johnny sprang off the bed, grabbed her, swung her round and I saw them bend together as he got his hand over her mouth. Then he humped the door shut, and there was silence again.

When one sees one's own dead spring into life like that, one does not normally rush about doing things. I just stood up there thinking, trying to see where the fault was in everything that had happened before.

There was no fault. Johnny was dead.

At the time I had been myself falling into what is artistically known as oblivion, with the blood leaving some areas of my inside where Johnny's bullet was. In such a state I might have been mistaken about Johnny's condition, but I was damned sure I hadn't been.

I am a good shot, what you might call as near an expert as you can get with ordinary practice at revolver shooting, and I knew where his organs were. So I knew where to shoot and how to shoot, and though he had got me first, I hadn't made any mistake. He was dead.

Then what kind of black magic was going on in that fantastic room down there?

Laura had screamed. She had been shocked, terrified. There was no faking a scream like that, nor that tigerish jump off the bed by the apparent zombie.

Several things puzzled me. Laura and I had talked together outside the door, surely the man inside the room must have heard us? If so, why did he still lie on the bed?

Or was that room soundproof? I remembered the small one next to it was, so the same might apply to the main one.

I listened. The water in the tank lapped softly and a loose bit of roof wood ticked in the slight breeze from outside.

There wasn't any sound from Johnny's room, so from what I knew of Laura's propensity for noise, the room must be pretty well sealed.

The ladder creaked a bit as I went down, but as I could hear nothing of them I reckoned they would hear nothing of me.

Very gingerly, I tried the door handle. It turned all right and the door gave. My instinct was to shove it open and rush in, but at that moment I heard someone coming up the passage behind me.

I shut the door again and turned back. I could see round the door jamb without being seen.

The lanky ruminant Fred was wandering

slowly along towards me, chewing, his hat on the back of his head. He appeared aimless but I knew him too well by now to think him that.

If that nose of his twitched, then there was nothing aimless about him.

I went out into the passage dead ahead of him. He stopped, stared at me idly and went on chewing.

'I think Laura's out,' I said.

'She was with you,' he said, and looked past me.

'That was some time ago. She went.'

His nose was twitching. He could smell the scent she wore. Laura was very liberal with scent and decorations.

He didn't believe me and his calm indifference to me was irritating. I decided to shatter his calm and see if I learnt anything from the shock.

'Johnny called for her.'

He stopped chewing, his nose stopped twitching. In fact, he seemed to stop altogether with his eyes on me like a couple of unset marbles.

'Johnny,' I said, as if jogging his memory. 'You remember Johnny?'

'He died.' Fred's Adam's apple slid up and down his thin neck. 'He died for sure, then!'

For a moment he seemed angry with his own bewilderment.

'Well, he's back, for all that,' I said. 'I wouldn't mistake him, would I?'

'You killed him, mister, that's a fact,' said Fred, starting to chew again. 'No mistaking that, then. Johnny's dead.'

'They must have invented something new down at the mortuary,' I said. 'He's alive, because I saw him, and Laura went with him.'

Fred wiped his face with an open, scraggy hand and looked at me afresh, as if to get a new angle.

'I don't know why you say that,' he said. 'There's no truth in it. A dead man can't be alive. They don't invent such things.'

'How has he come here, then?'

'You're mad,' said Fred, and spat on the passage floor. 'You don't make sense.' He scrubbed the spit out with his boot, looked at me, then turned and shambled away down the passage.

I had shaken him enough to push him aside from me, anyhow. He had gone away to think, or to discuss this affair with somebody.

That left me alone for a short time, though he might well bring somebody back.

I brought my pistol from my pocket and spent a half minute making sure it was in good order, because I felt I might need it very soon.

Then I took it in my right hand and tried the door again with my left. The lock turned easily, silently, it was well oiled. As I slid the door forward a quarter inch I reckoned I should have heard something from inside the room. I did, but it was a kind of soft sobbing.

I flung the door right back and went

after it so that anybody standing behind would have been fixed between it and the wall. But the handle crashed the plaster and a lot of door-knockers clacked and jangled.

My gun covered the room. Laura was sitting on the bed, tear-stained down her cheeks, but staring big-eyed at me.

She stopped sobbing and there was a silence.

There was no one in there but Laura and me.

In that moment of the shock I seemed to feel Johnny was truly dead. What I had seen was Johnny's earthbound spirit.

2

'Where is he, Laura?'

She started crying again and shook her head.

'Where is he?' I said.

'There is no one,' she said.

'Johnny!' I shouted.

She stared with big tearful eyes.

'Johnny's dead!' she protested and looked as if I had gone mad.

I sat on the bed beside her.

'Look,' I said, 'just now Johnny was in here, lying on the bed there, and he jumped up and grabbed you and slammed the door.'

She just sat and stared at me until I began to feel something had come adrift in my brain.

'Come off it, Laura,' I urged. 'You know he was here!'

'Johnny is dead,' she said, very slowly and hissing in her teeth. 'You shot Johnny dead. He cannot come here any more. The police took him away from the farm up there and he was buried. There is no Johnny any more.'

'But I saw him—here!'

She got up.

'I don't know what's the matter with you,' she said. 'You don't make sense.

You insist on looking up in the attic. All right, so I come in to turn down the bed. You want it turned down, don't you?'

'The door shut—' I began and watched the door shut itself. It was hung on rising hinges and was bound to shut, even when pushed flat wide, as I had done it. I grabbed desperately at another floating straw. 'If there is nobody here, what upset you? Why are you crying?'

She looked round.

'It all reminds me,' she said. 'Nothing has been changed, you see. It's all the same as when he was here.'

Well, that was a good explanation, too. The thing that shook me most was that I didn't believe Laura could act as well as this—this blank refusal to admit anyone was there.

Could it have been an illusion, a trick of the sight caused by the angle through the two openings?

But how in hell could you visualise a man who wasn't there?

'You screamed!' I cried.

'Me? What for?' She looked round blankly. 'You heard the door, then. Look—if it shuts quickly—' She pulled the door open again then shut it quickly and it gave a loud, grinding squeak.

I felt the sweat icing on my face. I began to have a definite feeling I was losing my grip on my reason.

'Your bag's there,' she said.

And then she went out leaving me in a room solid with silence.

I suppose one of the difficulties of going mad is that you refuse to believe you are. You don't believe you saw something that didn't happen; you go on trying to prove that it did.

The room hadn't been changed since I'd seen it last, the fantastic rows of door-knockers on the walls, the lewd pictures, little statues and books all were there, just as if Johnny were still alive.

'But he must be!' I said aloud. 'I saw him!'

But I knew damned well he couldn't be. Some things one knows for sure and I knew I had killed Johnny.

I sat on the bed and held my head in my hands, going over the whole of that mad scene again; Laura opening the door, the man on the bed, Laura screaming, the man springing up, getting her, twisting her round, gagging her as he slammed the door with his thigh.

It was all real.

Well, all right, do the Sherlock Holmes, I thought. Answer the impossible. If the man was here, forget who he was, just answer where was he? Where did he go?

I didn't know of any secret way in or out of this room, but remembering some of Johnny's activities it was quite likely that there was one.

And, come to think, what better disguise for a break in a heavily papered wall than a vast covering of glittering door-knockers?

That was one explanation, but suddenly I saw a much simpler one.

I had been up the passage for a minute or more, talking with Fred. During that time, a man could have come out of the door of Johnny's room and sneaked away.

That was easier than secret passages.

I went to the door to open it. It was locked fast.

So the quick slip-out looked the right answer. Laura wouldn't lock me in if there was another way out.

Leaning on the brass bedpost I reflected that I hadn't been very clever. As I looked back on things then I had to admit that I'd been damned stupid.

But I was locked in, and instead of wasting time being angry it seemed sensible to take a very close look round Johnny's room.

It was a rare old hodge podge, a Napoleon writing table, a Victorian bobble cover on the mantle, a couple of modern armchairs, a TV standing on a Roman imitation stool like a sectioned egg-cup, a couple of Sheraton chairs, a set of brass fire-irons hanging by the gas fire and a gas cylinder stuffed underneath a Victorian writing bureau.

Two pieces of writing furniture, yet the last thing I would have suspected among Johnny's activities was writing. But each had drawers and they could be interesting.

The Victorian bureau had a lot of papers, but they were all invoices and bills to do with goods bought for the pub. Johnny had gone out in a five ton truck of his own to buy everything for the inn. Whether this had been good business, or to keep brewers from sticking their noses in I did not know. At first I was surprised he had kept the accounts, but then I remembered he had been mean, and these records would be part of the miser act.

The Napoleon table was more interesting. There were a number of letters from people, obvious strangers to Dead End who wanted to stay for a day or two. All these had been refused and were marked so in a big, childish hand.

All these. I should have said, but two.

One I recognised as being from Janey, dated the previous November.

The other, dated a month before demanded two rooms over the dates September 2-5th, just about thirteen months before. It had been written by a secretary and signed by him or her. The address, unfortunately, and probably deliberately, was an hotel near Guildford, Surrey.

Now this didn't say who was coming. It just booked two rooms for the dates mentioned.

Yet careful, frightened, anti-stranger, xenophobic Johnny had accepted it.

Well, he must have known who it was and what it was for, and it was a sound bet to assume that Johnny had expected to make something out of it—something more than lodging fees, I mean.

My guess was that it must have been Alaski, or that it turned out to be him.

But if he had known that he must

have known Alaski. in which case there would have been no need for this formal booking.

It was rather odd. Johnny hated any strangers. He had thrown back every booking but two.

An idea struck me, but it was so fantastic that I just sat and thought about it for a while. Then I looked through all the booking letters again, the rejects and the two acceptances. They had all been marked in the big, childish hand in something I hadn't seen since a child—a blue pencil. The wording on the majority was 'Replied—No.' The remaining two were just marked, 'OK.'

There was but one common letter, an 'O' and they all looked the same to me. The only difference seemed a natural one. The starting 'O' had been begun at the bottom of the loop, but the one in 'No' had begun at the top, but then the 'N' finished at the top so that would be natural enough.

But when I tried it I found it very awkward to make an 'O' starting at the bottom, unless I did it with my left hand. Doing it as 'No' made no difference; you still began close to where the last letter finished, at the top.

Had Johnny been left handed?

I shut my eyes and recalled the only scene of him that might clue me: I pictured him once more at the door of the old larder, shooting at me with his pistol.

Such a recollection is very difficult to be sure of, but every time I shut my eyes and caught that scene again—and it was one I had every reason to remember—I could see the gun in his right hand.

Then something seemed to clinch it. For when I had fired back I remembered his free hand going for his middle, and his wrist watch had shown up there along with a big signet ring, an ornament such as the Johnny's breed delight in.

Of course, I realised I was just trying to prove my guess right; that somebody else, not Johnny had replied to the only two acceptances, some left-handed body.

I had the whole damned thing right there under my nose then, and I couldn't see it.

The warning about the door opening must have been instinct, for the sound-proofing prevented me hearing anyone coming outside.

I slid the old letters into the drawer and closed it. When the door opened I was sitting there looking out of the window.

Somehow I hadn't expected Lucia to be there in the opening. 'Don't let the door slam,' I said. 'It locks itself.'

She looked back at it, surprised.

'I don't see how,' she said.

'Let me look,' I said. When I saw it I saw a good mortise lock that could be unlocked from either side but could not slam shut. So Laura must have turned the key.

'Where's the key?' I asked her.

She shook her head.

'It wasn't locked.'

So somebody had unlocked it while I had been searching Johnny's drawers. The only reason I could think of was that locked, the key obstructed the view through the keyhole.

I was getting the creeps. These continued little pinpricks, digging into my mental security, were adding up. The phantom man, the locked door, the keyhole spy, Mrs. Chang in the altogether, they all had the same idiot lack of cohesion that made me feel I was going bonkers.

'Why did you come?' I said.

'Chang's going away.'

'Sudden?'

'I think it was you, or something you said or did. I do not know. He thinks a lot and says very little.'

'When's he going?'

'In an hour. He takes the two men. He always does that.'

'Bodyguard?'

'He has his reasons. He will be gone

until tomorrow afternoon.'

I sat on the bed and watched her.

'This gets loonier,' I said. 'He goes away leaving me, a highly suspected character, alone with his two women.'

'But women may watch,' she said.

'But what would they do?' I watched her placid, blonde features and the cold blue eyes. 'You are double-crossing him, and his wife—well, she isn't with him.'

'That is why I came to tell you,' she said.

'Lucia,' I said, 'I believe you're telling me the truth that you know. Myself, I smell a trick here. The false security, the sudden return, all these are familiar moves in the game.'

'But he must go and that is certain,' she said. 'The appointment is made. He must be there. It is unavoidable. I will give you the details.'

'There's plenty of time,' I said, looking past her to the door. 'Where's Laura?'

'Down there, getting food for you.'

'So she locked me in in case I tried to escape her care,' I said mockingly. 'Have you ever seen Johnny?'

She stared at me.

'You mean Johnny who was here? But no!' She laughed. 'He is dead. Because he is dead Chang is here. It wouldn't be so otherwise.'

'Well, I saw him,' I said. 'In this room, a half-hour ago.'

Her eyes grew very narrow.

'But there would be no reason for Chang to be here!' she said after a while. 'It is not possible. You must be wrong.'

'That's what we always say when nothing fits,' I said. 'But perhaps we are taking the bits in the wrong order, or the wrong way up. This is a mystery. If it wasn't we should see all the bits fitting in. But it seems they don't fit in. It is like opening a door and finding there is nothing the other side but empty air. That's what it seems like now. What we've got to do is accept the impossible.'

She laughed briefly. 'You'll go mad.'

'The way things have been so far, I'm there already,' I said. 'So there is nothing more to fear. Johnny is dead; Johnny was here. Chang can't go, Chang must go. Laura lied, but she can't act so she didn't. What she said was Laura's truth, but I saw the opposite happen. Why did she say there was no one there?'

'If you say it was dead Johnny then she must have been right.'

'Then again, switching,' I said, 'Chang must go in an hour. Why doesn't he want his secretary with him during the last minutes? Won't he wonder where you are? And if he does, won't he find out and suspect what you're up to?'

'He told me to tell you,' she said. 'It was almost as if he regards you as a bona fide developer.'

'That would be a nightmare twist,' I said.

'Perhaps you underestimate yourself,' she said. 'He taped what you said as you went round the house. It makes very interesting propositioning, imaginative, enthusiastic.'

Yet if Chang had been bamboozled it would explain something that was giving me the itch constantly. Ever since I had got into this place I had been expecting violence, great bursts of it, destroying explosions of it. All that had happened since the Land-Rover episode was nothing. Nothing at all.

I had gone the gamut of expectation; drugs in the Scotch, guns in my back, knives in my front, shadowing, threatening, the lush trap of beautiful Madame Chang —the lot.

And nothing had happened. No one had followed me, no one had hit me. Yet I felt more on the jump now than I had when I had come here before, and attempts on me and my future had chased each other like cigarettes down a packaging conveyor. It was the nothing that got me. The constant expectation, and the failure of it to appear was wearing me down.

It was as if I was tiring by being in a constant wrestling match against myself.

And perhaps, after all, that was part of the Oriental psychology.

That could be it.

On the other hand, I had found nothing to show Chang was a crook, and I couldn't remember anything that might make him think I was one. So he could be doing nothing because there was nothing he felt he ought to he doing.

Was I letting the old memories of Dead End get me into a nightmare that nobody else felt?

But there was Lucia, bold, cold Lucia who knew I was after something of value.

'What did you want me to do?' I said at last.

She shrugged.

'You have the run of the house now,' she said with a smile. 'Ferdi's room is empty.'

'Right,' I said. 'But suppose you have the wrong slant? Suppose what I want is not valuable in itself? Suppose it's just writing that will be a blackmail instrument?'

She shook her head, her eyes bright and pinpointed. She looked dangerous then.

'No, you are not the type,' she said. 'The fine, upstanding sporting type. No, no. You are out for prizes. This will be a prize.'

'You seem to know as much as I do,' I said. 'Because I tell you for sure I don't know what's there.'

'You are not such a fool!' She turned suddenly. 'I will be there.'

She went out. From the barred window I watched the road. I heard a buzz and a small car tore dust up the road, heading for the house.

I went to the door and opened it. There was a sound like a rat scuttering away. Instinctively I looked up towards the trap door in the ceiling of the boxroom.

There was a face, staring down. The shadow hid enough to disguise the features, and he drew back. I stood there, brushing my trousers with my hands, thinking what to do.

One thing I was not going to do was climb the ladder with that gentleman on top of me. My head is a delicate instrument.

I turned and went down the passage away from the bar, to the glass topped door at the end. Outside there had once been a wooden staircase running from the ground up to the attic, like a fire escape. Now, outside the door was nothing but a drop and the split remains of the wood brackets hanging out of the wall like old, tattered flags.

With the door open I stood on the brink and looked up. There were a lot of bits where the staircase had been wrenched away, and the door at the top was open, for I had seen it not long ago and since the crash it didn't fit the frame any more.

There was nobody below. There was nobody in the dusty fields.

My athletic training and practise makes

some things easy. I swung up from bracket to bracket as easily as if they had been rungs of a hand ladder.

When I came with my head level with the sill of the door I looked in. There was the man with his back to me, crouching, watching the open trapdoor.

It was easy. I almost laughed. I got a grip on the jagged remains of the old hand rail and lugged myself up until I could get my foot on the threshold.

Then he heard my foot shift on the gritty stone and spun round, his hand flung ahead of his face as if to defend himself against bright light.

I brought my revolver out, but he darted suddenly. He went behind a headland of slanting iron bedstead ends, curtain poles and lord knew what. It gave him cover to reach the next alcove. The long attic was sectioned into these alcoves, right up to the end where the big tank was.

I heard him moving, but couldn't see anything. I waited quite still in the hope that he would show, but he stopped moving altogether.

If there is one thing I am not mentally attuned for it is a waiting game. I begin to simmer, to boil, to hiss off steam and finally explode. I can't help it. It's my nerves.

I started forward. He must have been able to see me move for suddenly there was a rattling, groaning, shivering sound, and the stack of old bed ends and poles and iron bits and pieces began to heave up into a triangle like a pack of cards, then toppled over towards me, slithering and rattling and shuddering the place. Behind the rusty avalanche I saw him run out and duck for the trap.

He went down through it, just like a swimmer jumping into water, except that he didn't hold his nose when he went. I clambered round the iron mess, which wasn't easy, for any foothold gave way as iron slithered on iron and apart from bogging me down for a few seconds it made such a row I couldn't hear his flight.

Free of the obstruction and in the boxroom once more I listened. I could hear someone running, up towards the bar. I ran as lightly as I could along the passage.

As I came out on the landing overlooking the bar room, I saw him below me, running round the end of the counter, making for the private rooms of the inn.

I wanted him badly. I had the idea then, though I hadn't seen his face, that this was Johnny. If I got him, I would solve a mystery and the nervousness about my own sanity.

The landing rail was an easy vault down on to the big oak table in the middle of the room. I had done it before. It gained me yards, for as I rounded the counter I had the running man only a few yards dead ahead of me.

Then it happened; the Old Chinese Boot Trick, where your own eyesight clunks you right in the head and you don't know what you're looking at.

At the end of the passage there was a T-junction. The man reached it and split into two.

One of him ran to the right towards the yard, and the other ran to the left towards the other yard.

I just stopped. Anybody would. This was a culmination of a lot of tricks and the best one by far.

There had been Johnny who was dead, appearing upstairs. Now he had split, amoeba-wise, and there were two Johnnies, each running in a different direction.

The two men vanished at the ends of the passage and somewhere a door slammed and opened near me. Laura came out, breathing fast, running her hands up and down her thighs.

'What is it? What's happening?' she cried out.

'I'm going off my nut,' I said. 'Otherwise, everything's fine—'

I turned towards the T-junction to explain, when I saw it wasn't there any more.

The passage ran on for what looked like a quarter mile into the distance.

'Come in here!' she said. 'I want to talk to you!'

She grabbed my arm. I stared at her as, stunned, I went into the big old kitchen, of stone and beams and ceiling hooks. She slammed the door.

'That woman who came for you—' Laura said, her voice hissing in a half whisper as if she feared to be overheard.

'What about her?'

I shoved by and went to the kitchen door. It was open and looked into the yard, the bald, dusty, empty yard. Nothing moved there.

The split man had gone.

'She's a murderer!' Laura said.

I looked back at her.

'Who did she kill?' There was something about Laura's intensity that made me think she believed she was telling the truth.

Of course, as I pictured cold, bold Lucia, I had no difficulty in believing it. I could even see her doing it as a kind of clinical experiment.

Laura switched. 'Why were you running?'

'I was chasing a man,' I said.

'There was no man here,' she said. 'It was a woman!'

I was about to say she was cracked when it occurred to me I couldn't say she was wrong. Lucia had worn slacks when she had called, her hair was short and in the half darks, and split-action views I had had it might have been her.

'Who did she kill?' I said again.

'Alaski!' she hissed.

I stared at her a while. Then I whistled.

'I'm barmy,' I said. 'I've given under the strain. Get me a beer, Laura. I need a cooler.'

CHAPTER V

I

I had a drink, and while I did, I tried to trip Laura on one or two things that troubled me more than a jot. The man in the bedroom—Johnny. She kept on denying there had been one and I couldn't shake her. In the end she got angry about it.

'What the hell do you think I am, a dirty liar for nothing?' she yelled, all her gipsy blood boiling. 'Why the hell should I say there wasn't?'

'You've got a reason,' I said, not giving way.

'And you've got a dirty mind!' she cried. 'I don't know why I waste my time with you the way you behave. Always poking your nose in and bringing trouble on everybody else and then running off and letting everybody else suffer—'

'Forget it, Laura!' I said, outshouting her. She stopped from sheer shock of the noise. 'Where's Alaski?'

She stood rigid, and then flopped and let out a deep sigh.

'To hell with Alaski,' she said.

'He's probably there already, if what you say is true,' I said.

I watched her closely, because those few weeks back she had been Alaski's comfort when the brave politician had come to Dead End. Alaski had been quite a one for such comforts, but Laura seemed to have been a favourite of his. Seemingly, then, she should now show some bitterness or regret or some kind of personal emotion that he was dead.

The only emotion she showed was her usual flamboyant, kickaround sulkiness, which is hardly what I would have expected.

'It's true,' she said, pouting and turning away.

'If you know you must have seen him dead,' I said.

She whirled back on me, eyes and teeth flashing.

'Well, so I have, then!'

'Where did you see him?'

'Mind your business!'

'Now, look here, Laura. You've come clear of these jolly little jobs so far. You don't want to be hauled in as an accessory to a murder now, do you? When all the boil-up's done? You'd be crackers. This is the time to clear everything up.'

'Why do you want to see him, then?' she demanded.

'I want to be sure he's dead,' I said, and decided to give her time to think. 'Get me another beer, Laura.' As she took my glass and went to the door, I threw out, 'Better tell me, then I can tell the police. Otherwise they'll come pumping you. That won't be nice.'

She hissed contemptuously and went out. She was a long time gone. I began to suspect she was up to something, but she came back in again with a fresh drink.

'There's a vault back of the chapel,' she said.

'There?' I queried. 'In a vault? But that's very considerate. Such a saving! How do you know?'

'I saw them, one night,' she said. 'That woman—she was standing up, giving orders. Ferdi and the other man, the Arab, they were putting him down there.'

It wasn't hard to guess at the reasons and what-have-you. Alaski had told Chang something in Singapore, Chang had come to make use of it for himself, Alaski had risked a return at some cost to himself and paid the final price by turning up in Dead End.

'How do you know it was the woman?' I said.

'I heard the shot. They walked him out to the garden. I could see because of the moon. I heard them talking, and she was behind him. She fired. I saw the flame, right behind him, and the other two ran and caught him. Then she gave them orders to go on.'

She was breathing hard, staring out of the window as if at some distant, nightmare scene. Then I sensed her feelings were something more than she had shown.

It seemed I was wrong about her acting. She could act a bit after all.

'You've been keeping quite a secret, Laura,' I said.

She sat down on the bench beside me and looked at me. She had tears in her eyes now.

'I had to tell somebody,' she said. 'It was burning in me, like a pain. You're not a bad fellow. I don't think you dare tell the police, anyway.'

'Thanks for the confidence,' I said, and laughed.

She felt better, or looked it and dabbed

her eyes on my tie. I laughed again, amused this time.

I had a mind then to thump in that one about Johnny in the bedroom again, but I could feel it would do no good, and might lose me a confidante. Johnny would have to wait.

'I'll go back there,' I said. 'And look around for you as I promised.'

'There must be money there,' she said.

She turned as there came a banging and calling from the bar.

'All right, I'll come !' she yelled, then stood up. 'You come back and tell me, then,' she added to me.

'I'll be back,' I said, and added to myself, 'I surely hope.'

She went out. After a moment or two, I followed her and turned right, down to where the fugitive had split in two.

It was all very easy when you saw it. I just walked down the passage and met myself walking from the other way. First time, that mirror could not have been quite shut, for it had shown the passage but not myself and Laura at the kitchen door. Now it was fully shut.

I shoved the cold surface and it swung back. The reflection of the angled passage swung round, too, and the hinged mirror stopped, showing a perfect reproduction of the passage into the sunny yard.

I pulled the mirror open again. The mirror had been fixed on a cupboard door.

'And what the hell for?' I muttered.

Granted, it was an old mirror, stripped off an old wardrobe up in the attic, perhaps, but why shove it on here? I had helped my fugitive get away solely because of the shock of seeing him—or her—split into two.

Another Chinese trick? I remembered some conjurer on the stage long ago who used the catch-phrase 'all done with mirrors.'

Suddenly I wondered if Johnny in the bedroom could have been done that way.

Some kind of flash reflection on a backless mirror—

Reflection from where? There wasn't another bedroom nearby, only the box-room.

And I had seen him grab Laura. I was sure of that, no matter what she said.

I went out into the yard and looked around. The old, familiar rubbish laid about, the old sheds and stables with wide-split, unpainted wood, lurching doors, gaping water butts and the heap of planks which had been the garage I had pushed over with my car weeks ago. Nobody had touched it since, nor anything else for that matter.

Up and down the village there was nobody about but a bobtailed dog lying in the road his face on the ground, staring unwinkingly at me.

I heard a car coming, a soft, sandy sound of big tyres on the gritty road. The Mercedes came past the corner of the building laying a dust trail behind.

The dog jumped up and scampered in at a broken gateway. The big car went on towards the winding, climbing track up out of Dead End.

Chang was on his way. My way, then, was theoretically clear.

Perhaps I have a suspicious nature, but in places like Dead End I get uneasy about open doors and gates and lack of secret supervision. I don't like it. It always looks like old cheese in a mousetrap, and smells. Of course, they say if you have something wrong with your brain you can smell things that aren't there. Perhaps that was it. Kidding, of course.

The gun was heavy in my pocket, pleasantly heavy.

There I was going again. Nobody had hit me, chased me, shot at me, threatened me and the Land-Rover could have been an accident or a sudden urge by a rattlebrain seeing himself once more jostling a hated rival off the tracks.

Somebody had been in the attic and run

away. Well, why did that have to do with me? Was I getting a persecution complex, or was this a Chinese method to make me create my own dangers?

I started walking out among the bushes and the small trees of a wood. Water bundled down a rocky fall, cutting little rainbows across the green background. Beyond it stood the deserted basin of the stone quarry.

I had almost a nostalgia as I clambered over the whitish rocks and looked down across the clear space to the tumbled rock over the old entrance to the workings. From there they had cut a direct tunnel to the Germ Station, and had nearly got what they had long planned to get when my dynamite charges blew up and fired the whole explosive store.

Luck, sheer damn luck. Bad for them, just in time for me.

I sat on a smooth stone and stared across the white ground, hot still, though the sun was hitting the hill ridge on the western side of the circling hills.

The old rail tracks snaked across to the heap of fallen stone and vanished under it, smothered. A line of white, rust-stained trucks stood away to my right. Beyond them the trees of the house garden lurched over the crumbling bricks of the garden wall.

I saw someone move across one gap in the wall, but did not see who it was. According to Lucia it could have been herself or Madame Chang. There shouldn't have been anyone else there.

The tumbled entrance to the workings fascinated me, as the scene of a great disaster. I went across to it and stood looking at the ruins. The evening birds were a long way off. It was very quiet there. I felt an odd chill in the sun's long shadow.

The thing gleamed in the dusk, catching the high light of the sun, shining up from between two tumbled stones on the rail line.

I crouched and picked it out of its dusty grave. Then the chill in me froze all my muscles.

What I held was the actual signet stone, with its engraving gold lined, of the ring which Johnny had worn.

There could he no mistaking it, for every detail of that last picture of his dying and my nearly following were on my memory now for good.

The stone was a squared oblong, and had been in a gold setting. I looked around the dust but found nothing of the ring and setting. This stone must have been somehow torn out, possibly by the explosion—

Good God, no! Impossible! Johnny had not been in the explosion, he had been tracking me to the farm. And anyhow, I had seen him wearing the ring after the blow up.

Then how had it got here?

As I had been told and guessed for myself, after that double shooting in the farmhouse, the police had got there within minutes and had taken over. They had taken Johnny to the mortuary and me to the operating theatre.

Well, Johnny must have been wearing the ring to the morgue—what did they do then? Take off his jewellery and give it to his mother? What do they do? Do they bury them with rings on?

I didn't know what they did, but guessed they would take them off and shovel them in to the next of kin, or in accordance with the conditions of a will.

I slipped the stone in my pocket and walked back to the inn. There were a few men in the bar and they all stopped talking when I went in. When I went to the bar, they all went away from it and sat down at tables, watching me.

It was the same atmosphere of silent menace I remembered from before. Laura didn't like it.

'You want your supper?' she said. She wanted to get me out of that room before anything happened.

'Might as well,' I said.

'Come in the kitchen. It's ready,' she said, as she turned and went out down the passage.

I followed her and was surprised to find she had got me a cold meal, covered over with an old fashioned meat safe of gauze.

'I thought you'd gone to the chapel,' she said.

'I'm on my way,' I said. 'But you made me hungry. Look.' I opened my hand and showed her the stone.

'Seen that before?'

She looked at it, then looked at me.

'Johnny's,' she said.

'That's what I thought,' I said. 'How does it come like this? Have you got the ring?'

'It was in his room,' she said. 'There is a writing table. In one of the drawers. Somebody must have taken it out.'

'The police gave it to you?'

She nodded.

'Somebody stole the gold and threw the stone away,' she said. 'It wouldn't have been any good, the stone. It was a special—special sign. It would have been recognised.'

'Johnny's father?'

She stared at me a while, defiant, and yet faraway, as if remembering something.

'Yes,' she said. 'His father.'

It was a pity. I had hoped there would be a lead here, but stealing a ring for the gold was a sound story, specially when the thief threw the identifying stone away.

She signed towards the meal and went out. I sat down. I would sooner wait till dark, or near it.

Just how did one, a casual thief, tear a stone out of a ring? With a penknife? It would take some doing.

Of course, it could have been wrenched out. And how? By accident. By the wearer digging down between those stones to find something, and catching the ring between two rough surfaces and tearing it out.

Simple.

But who would have been wearing it after Johnny? Who would have risked being identified by a stolen ring?

It seemed only Johnny would wear it—could wear it—without bringing misery on his head.

Yet Johnny had died wearing it.

We were back amongst the zombies again.

2

As I ate I laid the stone on the scrubbed table and looked at it. The sign could have been a scorpion, but it was a hell of a fanciful one, and might have been an Oriental land crab or something.

Oriental. I looked at it more closely and decided it could well have been so exotic. Well, well! There was a link with the East, with Singapore with Alaski and Chang—if my guess was right.

When she came out for something I said, 'What was Johnny's father?'

She looked at me briefly.

'An airman,' she said, and walked out.

Well on the plains of Wiltshire there used to be quite a few airfields and there are some left, one in particular, still a big trooping field, flipping troops to all over the world, but mostly Eastwards of home.

Reckoning on Johnny having been twenty, that would bring his father back to when a hell of a lot of troops were being flown back from the East in bombers and transports. I heard a lot of stories of the stuff the boys used to smuggle back in the bomb bays. They became, for a little while, merchants of a kind. They had some high times, trying to smuggle ten yard square Indian carpets off the dispersal points and past the guards.

Pilots on those runs could have made valuable contacts, one or two such airmen might have held on and made something of those contacts later. But as the contacts had been fishy to start with, they very likely went on faintly in the shade.

Things began to roll out smoothly. The pilot based at a nearby airstrip taking comfort from Laura, a fine, bright but very young Gyppo girl, and leaving her at last with a fine bouncing boy to keep her company during his own travels East—

But wait. There had been Linda as well. Linda perhaps, nineteen, which meant in any case that Laura had fallen for the same talk twice.

Yet Laura, hot blooded as she certainly was, didn't seem the sort to fall for it twice without grabbing hold of the sportive donor and holding on.

Which brought me to a point which had never failed to surprise me: how young Laura looked and behaved when she had children of nineteen and twenty. At most, I had never thought her motherhood could have started later than fifteen in order to work the sum out and adjust it with her physical beauties.

I made up my mind to take advantage of one of the amenities of Dead End, if I could find him.

It was getting dusky when I went out by the passage into the yard. There was a rumble of talk from the open bar door, and I went right round, through the yard and out on to the road that way.

Whenever I had seen Fred the Nose he had been leaning or lounging around the end cottage which butted on to the field which had a monument of a rusty tractor in the corner.

I was lucky. He was sitting up on the rusted tractor saddle, whittling wood and staring around him, his head going to and fro on his thin neck like a radar scanner. When he saw me it got stuck in my direction, his hands went on with the whittling motions.

It was easy to walk through the broken fence. He went on staring till I came up to the tractor and leant on the iron rim of a rear wheel.

151

'You didn't find Johnny?' I said.

'Johnny's dead,' said Fred and stopped shaving his bit of wood.

'Well, all right,' I said. 'Do you remember when he was born?' He stared at me and his nose twitched. 'Look, I don't want to go on being bad friends. I've nothing against you. Whatever I did was only accident. I just travel in beer. You have some with me.' I gave him a fiver and waited.

He looked at it, looked at me, then looked towards the pub and grinned like a skull. Then he took the note, stuffed it into a pocket of his unbuttoned waistcoat and went on sawing at his wood.

'He weren't born here,' he said, watching his work.

'I thought she said he was.'

'No. She came with two kids. Stayed there—' he shook a shoulder towards the inn, '—and said she was awaiting her husband. Well, he never come. Ted had pub then, and he was dead hard up, war being over and the troops all gone from around, and he was going to throw her out and sell up.'

Fred began to laugh quietly to himself.

'Well, she upped and bought the pub off him, so some money must've turned up from somewheres. Knocked us all, that did. Must be twenty year ago, I s'pose. I were not twenny myself, then. God, she were a beautiful girl. Still is.'

'But she wasn't very old?'

'No. Younger'n me. Long ways younger. Childbride they called her, though twere a wonder she didn't have some more, kids, I mean. But she were young all right, but you couldn't tell. These Gyp kids develop quick and she was developed all right and had the sauce of the devil. Come to think, she seemed old enough then, but now she don't. She hadn't got old enough now.'

'But the kids looked like her.'

'Gyppos all looks the same to me.' He chipped away.

'But the pub went down.'

'Aye that went down. What else? There's no trade. She never seemed to care, and then Johnny took over, like, and that's when money started to come in, like.'

He meant when Alaski's ideas had begun to impinge upon the village. Yet, the tunnel must have been planned and most of the work done before that letter came booking the rooms, which I was sure had come from Alaski.

If that was Alaski's first visit, then who had organised the vast engineering project before that? This was the first time I realised that the booking and the workings through the hills just did not coincide.

Fred said a little more, but nothing that was not adding to what he had said. He was trying to earn a fiver. Next minute, if somebody offered him another fiver, he would unhesitatingly nose me out so that I could be shot. At least, one was never not knowing where one stood in Dead End.

I walked on towards the House, strolling. When I came to the lodge I went in and looked around in the gloom. I also looked out of the windows to see who was about.

Once more I saw somebody moving, this time crossing the overgrown drive. The dusk was growing and in the overhung drive the light was too bad for me to see who it was.

After a short time I came out of the lodge and turned in amongst the bushes, heading for the old chapel. Three times I stopped and waited, looking back, but saw no one, and I went on to the chapel.

It was a good scene for a wild film, the old stone rearing up out of the skeleton hands of ivy and switching trees, the lolling tombstones, the great grim doors with their grinning hinges splitting them across, and the big ring handle rusting in the middle.

The padlock was as big as a birthday cake with a keyhole you could get your finger in. It was old, but it hadn't been out in the weather all that long. It looked as if it had been brought out of preservation for the job.

Once more I peered around in the gathering dusk, but saw no one about. I went to the doors and examined the lock. Then I went all the way back to the lodge. I was in no hurry, and I wanted one of the slim wire hooks that were fixed to the window shutters. I wrenched one off and returned to the chapel, quite sure then that no one followed me.

Having many friends amongst the police and the gentlemen they do business with, I know some tricks about picking locks. You just have to know how a lock works and have some patience. The last I hadn't got, but I forced myself.

Wonderful for me, I stuck it for ten minutes and at the end of that time, had it undone. The half door groaned like a lost soul when I pushed it open. It was dark as hell inside.

My little torch was hardly big enough for such a vasty void as I shone it into. In fact it was just a too bright little diamond floating in space, but then I managed to make out the side of a pew, and my way along it over the worn, dished flags.

Something made me stop and look back, but I could see no more than the grey crack of the parted doors. I turned the light off and stood listening.

The wood of the place creaked with the changing temperature of evening. The fingers of a tree touched a window restlessly, and my eyes could just make out the tall shapes of stained glass windows, dark with dirt and the dusk, half blocked by the wandering arms of trees.

Then I saw I had made a mistake in using the torch at all. The dazzling spot had prevented my eyes getting used to the deep gloom. It was gloomy, make no mistake. I could see better if I did not look at a thing, but slightly above it.

That was the way I thought I saw a face, a pale blob in the darkness where some sort of metal props shone a little.

I stopped and tried to make out what it was. I distinguished the metal props as candlesticks, ranged up in size like organ pipes.

The blob face was behind them, as if peering between the brass stalks.

I felt the back of a pew and stepped into it, so as not to be in the line of the door. With my eyes on the blob I felt in front of me and found nothing. I was standing with my back to the front of the first pew.

Again I listened, holding my breath, but the creaking and the switching of the trees against the glass defeated my aim.

The blob seemed to move slowly sideways, but I could not be sure. I fixed the upright candlesticks in my sight, stood dead still and watched.

I saw the blob move very slowly sideways away from me. For a long time it was bisected by the vertical candlestick, then it moved until it had drifted clear.

The smell of the air was cold and musty. I wished I had Fred the Nose with me; he would have found in a moment if there was a living man there—or even a dead one.

My eyes began to cheat with the steady strain of trying to make out what they couldn't. There just was not enough light to see and too much small sound to let me hear.

Then the big door groaned.

It was only part of a sound, as if something had brushed it and made it move on the hinges a fraction, but it was enough.

The evening was not still, but there was not enough air to have moved that great plank of a door.

I looked round. Nothing moved against the tall grey strip of light at the opening, but I didn't like it. Anything could have made the door grunt, perhaps, but I feared people and I fixed on people.

At my left I made out the upright of a stone pillar. I touched it and moved in beside it. I looked back at the blob behind the candlesticks. It was still there, but seemed to have moved closer towards me since the groaning of the door.

It was still shapeless but seemed to be shedding a very faint halo of light round it. In that moment it seemed that everything was still but the slowly moving blob.

The trees had stopped scratching, the beams of the building were settled and creaked no more. Yet something creaked, and again I thought it was the big door.

But even as I looked towards it I realised that the sound had come from my right, and not from the doorway.

I looked back towards the blob. It seemed to be moving, again very slowly but away from me once more.

To me, from me, very, very slowly. It had a pattern which was not that of a live thing.

My curiosity was getting the better of me, tempting me to put caution aside to see what the damned thing was.

I looked back towards the door. The long grey slit was untouched by any shadow, but a tree finger, suddenly touching a stained glass panel, made me jump.

There wasn't any other sound for a while, then the little squeaky groan again from near the blob.

I went forward, feeling for the edge of the rise with my soft shoe. I found it and felt my way ahead by the stone pillar. I wanted to get behind the screen of candlesticks.

At this point I had the strong feeling that the blob was somebody and that they did not know I was there. What gave me that idea I don't know, but I had the feeling whoever was there was asleep.

I crept along. The blob became less faint, but its shape became more confusing than ever, something like two small, thin faces close together. The little squeaky groan came again, close to me now and somehow over my head so that I looked up into pitch darkness.

Then in the blackness I saw a vertical greenish light, a tiny glowing strip, bright in the darkness. Then, as the blob seemed to turn away the light vanished.

It was like a luminous watch face caught side on for an instant as it turned away.

Then in the gloom I made out the shape of the blob at last.

They were a pair of white canvas shoes, turning very slowly at about the level of my chest. The little squeaky groan was a rope twisting and untwisting very slowly.

3

There was a sound from somewhere now that could not be mistaken; footfalls. They were slow, but definite, approaching the chapel along the overgrown path.

I got back away from the hanging man and walked into a candlestick. It rocked and I caught out at it to stop it clattering over.

Quite suddenly I had an appalling thought. There I was in this place with a hanging man, and any time now the police would come round on their nightly visit.

Suppose this was one of Laura's tricks?

She had got me into the chapel knowing a cadaver would be swinging from the roof beams. If I was caught with this lot, a gun in my pocket and a motive—

The motive stuck in my mind, for I had seen only one man wearing white canvas shoes in Dead End.

Ferdi had been wearing them in his room that afternoon. The room where we had fought.

Chang would, of course, bear witness that I believed Ferdi had tried to kill me in the Land-Rover.

The footsteps came to the door and stopped.

CHAPTER VI

I

The footfalls stopped, and there was only the slow, faint creaking of the rope to be heard in the darkness. After a moment there were two or three more steps outside, and then silence again.

The steps were quite loud, as if the walker did not know—or care—that there was someone in the chapel.

I came out from behind the candle range, keeping my eyes on the strip of the open door. As I halted I heard someone muttering outside, an irritated, impatient sound; someone swearing at himself—or herself?

Then there were two more steps, louder than the others, treading the grass-broken stone of the chapel path. They came to the open doors and now one of them groaned. It was a different sound from any I had heard since I had come in, a quick, pained grunt, as if the pusher had used some force.

I could see a shadow against the grey strip of evening, and went behind the stone pillar.

Almost instantly, a brilliant beam of light flashed along the aisle from the doors. Instinctively I closed my eyes, then used the dimmer of my lashes to watch the solid beam of light.

It stayed still for seconds, blazing back off the dull brass candlesticks, turning them into white gold. Dust whirled in the beam. A many-pronged fork of candles blazed blackly up the wall behind the altar.

The light moved slowly, over towards my pillar. It moved across the bulk of stone, the beam moving on either side of me, trying to feel out my shoulders.

It changed direction and went back slowly across the candles, then struck the slow turning shoes.

It stopped abruptly, picking the shoes out. Then the beam began to climb the body, legs, the dangling hands, the loose arms, and then up to the gross, bloated face, a white blaze of horror against the arches of the roof trusses.

The light clicked out. I waited. Shoes gritted on the step, turning, then steps began to walk away.

I went quickly out of my hiding and along the aisle to the door opening. Through it I could see someone walking away, slowly, even thoughtfully. It could have been man or woman. The light was too dim and confused to be sure.

There was a decision to he made; to go on with what I was looking for, or to follow and find out who the person had been.

The behaviour was odd enough, night-marish, really, when you think the watcher had explored a newly dead man with a light, and then just turned and walked away, unmoved, it might seem.

I was left alone in the silence—that is, save for the slow twisting creak of the rope.

The slight movements of the trees seemed to be easing right away into the absolute still of evening. I turned and went back along the aisle to the altar. I used my small torch, and it seemed to throw a more definite light now that it had objects to reflect on.

Like the overturned chair underneath the slowly turning canvas shoes. There was little I could tell from it. It might have been a suicide's seat, or put there to make it look like one.

According to Chang, Ferdi had been a nerve-broken nut, and such lost characters can do things like this, given rope, a chair and an unfightable depression.

It would all have fitted. My own nervous suspicion just wouldn't let it, that was all.

There was a door to the left behind the

hanging man. I looked at it, then back at the corpse. My instinct was to cut it down, but I was afraid my instinct would land me in too much trouble, if I should leave a lot of marks identifying myself with Ferdi's demise, so I left him.

The door was in good shape. The handle had been used and worked easily. It led through into a small room, a vestry, I guessed and a little later I knew. For there was a big book on a sloping top desk.

Opening it I found the parish records, as one might call them, though they dealt only with Dead End village and the Manor House.

Of necessity, there weren't many entries, for there had not been many people ever in Dead End. I let the stiff, yellow pages flip off my finger until I came to the blanks. Then I looked back to where the entries finished half-way down a page.

The last entry was in dead black ink and shone out against the faded style of the rest.

'Johnny Burnlow,' I read, followed by the words, 'Shot dead at Upward Farm,' and then the date I had shot Johnny. It was a shock, like frozen blood suddenly pouring in my veins. It seemed like an indictment, no worse, a judgement.

Recently entered in a characterless sort of writing, comparing badly with the educated flow of the rest of the entries.

There was no other Burnlow as far back as I could see.

A further fact was that I had never heard the name before. Laura hadn't used it, and I had never heard Johnny called anything but Johnny plain and unattached.

Well, somebody with a strong sentimental feeling had come and made this entry, and I was sure it hadn't been Laura, for if she had been able to get in, she would have spent her time looking round for treasure hidden there by Johnny not in writing his name and final history in the records.

She hadn't got in there. Was it because

she couldn't beat the padlock, or because she was too scared?

There was an uncomfortable feeling inside me that I had all the pieces of the puzzle in my hands, and that if I put them together right I could collect what I had come for and walk out of Dead End whole.

But I couldn't fit them together. I couldn't see the shape of each item of evidence because I couldn't judge its importance.

Some things fitted. Ferdi fitted. Take his story that he had a return-to-the-past brainstorm in the Land-Rover, ditching me and getting himself treated with contempt by Chang and the rest. In his state of mind he could have hanged himself.

That read straight. There was just one thing I had to make out before I passed it.

I went all round the chapel with my little light. The only other door out of the place, apart from the main ones, was at the end of the little vestry. I drew the bolts, turned the handle, but it wouldn't come.

That one, too, must have been padlocked outside.

Well, then, so Ferdi was murdered. Unless he had got in some way outside the doors. I couldn't see anywhere, but that didn't prove there wasn't one.

The vestry claimed my attention again, for the records book proved someone was recently there. Then I remembered Laura's story of the shooting by the vaults entrance.

'At the back of the chapel,' I thought she'd said.

Well, the vestry was at the back end, balancing up an organ chamber on the other side of the nave. In fact, these two bits made the formal plan of the cross.

The vestry was on the side away from the house, thus could be 'the back'.

As I was trying to sort out these things the continual slow creak of the rope kept seizing my bowels in a small cramp of horror. It kept making me feel I ought to cut the wretch down.

I looked round the floor of the vestry, bending to get my little light right down on the cracks in the boards. I was wrong. There wasn't a hole in the boards, but there was one in the back of the vestment cupboard. It opened out quite easily. An old bolt hole so that the priest could get out before the soldiers arrived, or some such. Could it be as old as that?

There were some brick steps going down inside, though I had to bend up pretty well, the going being only four feet high.

It smelt awful, like being buried in mould, or even manure; a gust of horrid odours rushing up as if they had been waiting in the tunnel to get out.

I went down, my little light seeming quite bright, and I came into the five foot high room of a vault. Coffins lay on slate shelves around it, old coffins, half a dozen of them, none new.

Nor was there any new cadaver.

I looked all round the grim long boxes and the steps up to the sealed door of the vault from the outside.

Alaski was not there.

I went to the outer stone door. It was well secured by some means from the outside. I don't know what sort of locks they have for vault doors. I had never before been so close to a vault of this particular kind.

The investigation of the stone door showed a lot of scratches and what looked like bloodstains dragging down the stone, as if someone had tried to claw a way out.

The thought gave me the shivers and I turned back to the way I had come in. That, too, must have a cover for its obvious exit. The mourning relatives would never have allowed a way out to the dear departed.

The thing was sticking out in front of me like a wing of stone, a buttress sticking out from the wall. I could not see how it was pivoted but it moved very easily, a masterpiece of engineering balance. There was a large bolt on the tunnel side.

The coffins fascinated me as well as frightened me. Some were ornate in iron bindings, and one of these caught my eye, for there were bright silver scratches on the iron straps by the lid.

I looked round the other coffins, but none of the others bore signs of having been interfered with. I shifted the one near the tunnel so that I could see a bit behind it, but spotted no marks. I left it where it was and went back to the scratched one.

My new examination was just playing for time. I just couldn't bring myself to get the lid off and look into the rotting remains of some long dead lord of Dead End.

The lid lifted when I got the rim of my gun muzzle under the iron edge of one of the straps. Then I faced up to the horrors within and just shoved the lid up till it clacked against the wall.

I could have seen light there without the

use of my little torch. For the single beam bounced back a million times, burning with multicolour fire, flashing like the dazzling splinters of lightning, glowing with the inner fire of stone and rare concretion of nacre. A pirate's treasure burning in the secret darkness of death.

The crash behind me was like a shot. I swung round. The stone escape door was partly shut, only jammed on the corner of the coffin I had left in its way.

A hand was trying to push the coffin back so the door would close.

Suddenly I knew the meaning of the bloody clawmarks on the other door and I jumped. I got the other end of the coffin just as the pusher got it clear. The door would have shut but I grunched the box forward in time. Once again the door jammed on it.

My torch fell and went out. I heard somebody breathing and felt the terrific pressure of his pushing the coffin against me.

My whole strength and the power of sheer terror shoved against the attempt to bury me alive. I felt it grunt against me harder, a half inch win for him.

My foot got the edge of the opposite shelf and I shoved hard. For a moment I won an inch, then two, then gradually I felt my advance stop and the box began to come back against me.

I let it come for a few awful seconds, gathering my strength, and then I pressed forward with every bit of every muscle. I felt no give. It was as if I pushed against a wall. The more strength I gave the more pain began to shoot through my muscles as they cracked and tore against the immovable weight.

Then it gave, suddenly. The coffin shot forward, crashed against something soft. I heard a gasp, then the box struck stone and the shock came right back through me.

It winded me, and through the sear of pain in my ears I heard somebody trying to run up the steps, panting. There was despair and lameness in that sound.

I bent and tried to find the torch. I got it at last, flicked it on and pushed the coffin skew-whiff back on its shelf.

The stairs were empty, but I could hear the gasping, the dragging of a foot somewhere above me. The roof of the little tunnel was too low for any speed to be made up the brick steps.

I took it easily, with the torch out. But the sounds of the overtaxed friend ahead of me were clear and some distance ahead.

I got into the vestry and heard someone in the body of the church. Then the sounds stopped abruptly.

There was a glow of yellow light coming through the open vestry door. I went to the edge of the opening and peered through.

Several of the candles were burning, their flames wavering slightly from the draught of someone passing, but steadying even as I watched.

The man's slowly turning shoes were on my right. I could see beyond the candle glow to the main doors, and the range of empty, ghostly pews.

The rope creaked, gave a little scream, then cracked and parted. The sacklike corpse hit the ground with its feet, its knees folded, and the whole body sagged into a a heap, turned over and tumbled to a halt, looking up at me, its eyeballs out like boiled eggs, its tongue sticking out, the whole face distorted, somehow bloated, hardly recognisable.

But even with the horrible distortion I saw this was not Ferdi.

This was one-time master crook Alaski.

2

Alaski could never have strung himself up. He had left most of his fingertips smeared down the stone door of the burial vault.

I dislike violence. I am sick with unpleasantness. Alaski made me feel sick then, he was such a mess.

And what made me feel sicker was that if I hadn't been able to shove that damned coffin a bit harder than the other chap, it would have been my fingertips being worn out now, as my panicky, claustrophobic head had its screaming way.

A wave of sweating fear passed through me then, and I stayed where I was behind the door jamb. I reckoned my friend would not come to me, but was waiting somewhere in the chapel.

Alaski had been cut down. I could see the sprouting end of the rope where it had been cut. There was nothing for a cutter-downer to stand on, but there was quite a length of rope trailing off Alaski's neck. So it had been cut near the roof beam.

My friend must have got up there and cut the rope from above.

Well, he hadn't come down.

I began to feel better. With my eyes on the door opening I got my revolver out and fingered it. The motion was very strengthening. My diaphragm was still sore from the way my friend had shoved the coffin into it.

A stray thought came into my head as I stood there waiting.

It was that in the treasure coffin there was enough to keep a man for life—if he could find a means to lug it away. Magog would be worth as much, but was more portable.

But I didn't know where Magog was. This was a case of a bird in the coffin being worth Magog in a bush. But then again, there was the carriage problem. I felt like Midas trying to eat a bun.

One thought I had didn't even need to be thought; that treasure was Johnny's. How he had come by it I hadn't time to think, but it was the bait which had brought Chang and the return of Alaski—

But if so, why hadn't Chang got it?

He couldn't have found it, or he wouldn't have pushed Alaski down there with it.

Then it occurred to me what he wanted me for. If he watched me, secretly, while I thought I was having a free hand, then he might find places in the house and outhouses that he didn't know but thought I would, or would find.

But this was no time to work out problems. My friend was up in the beams looking down on the vestry door, and that door was my only way out.

How to see up into the roof without a knife skimming down and cutting my head off was the immediate theorem for solving.

My head performed a computer chain. Chang—spying—tricks—mirrors.

I looked back to where a small old mirror hung on the wall by the cupboard door, the clergy face-adjuster, spotted now with age and neglect, but mirrorwise all the same.

It came easily off the wall. I moved very quietly and came back to the doorway. It was essential not to let my periscope catch the candlelight, so I gave it a reverse angle to the radiation, but that showed the beam against the end wall, and nobody on it. I shaded the edge of the mirror from the candles and traversed the roof slowly. It meant holding the gun in my left hand, but there is bound to be a disadvantage when the opponent has the advantage. I can't shoot left-handed. I can't do much left-handed.

These thoughts flashed in me when the mirror caught something odd amongst the beams of the roof truss directly above the door.

It was the steely spark of a knife blade, and as I steadied the mirror I saw it was gripped in a man's left hand.

The mirror was quite steady, but so was he. The beam he stood on hid him almost completely. I put the mirror on the sloping desk and got my gun in my right hand. Then I squeezed up to the edge of the door jamb.

'Better come on down, matey,' I said. 'I've got a gun on you, and it's loaded.'

Silence. I might have been speaking to myself like a child at play.

'If you don't come down,' I said, 'I'll shoot your hand off as a piece of advice.'

Squinting up I could see the hand with the knife. It contracted and disappeared above the big beam.

Then there was a movement, the last one I expected.

The roof trusses were eight or ten feet apart right down to the end. The man suddenly strode out from one to the next, sprang off that to the next. It was like watching a giant striding, and perspective blocked my chance of a shot at him, each beam he left covered half his back.

I ran out, for he had to come down at the end.

When he came on to the last truss but one he turned from the waist and slung the knife backhanded. I saw it flashing towards me in the candlelight, and twisted aside. It was a good shot. It ripped my shirt sleeve as it went by and struck one of the candlesticks. One tottered, hit another, the flames started dancing as the tall brass things rocked together, and then like skittles, they rocked too much and went over. The lights sputtered, smoked and died.

I ran on again into the sudden darkness, seeing nothing, but ready to grab. I hit the edge of a pew and felt I had broken my thigh bone. It steadied me up and I stopped.

I heard something ahead of me, soft footed on the stone of the step. I began to see the grey of the open door, but nothing blocking it.

It sounded as if he had got out on to the step and was waiting for me there. I crept on towards the faint sound, a soft shiffing, as if he, like a boxer, was moving his feet in the resin.

Then suddenly a shadow formed across the opening. I grabbed it by one shoulder and stuck the gun in what I thought was its back.

But it was a silken middle.

'Why do you do that?' the small voice said. 'I only come to find if you are hungry.'

I let go, let the gun fall to my side, fumbled and found my little torch.

'It's a funny thing, Madame Chang,' I said, 'but I'm not a bit hungry. I was talking with somebody. Did you meet anyone?'

'There was no one,' she said, without emotion. 'There never is.'

'No,' I said. 'Perhaps you're right there.'

My second private meeting with her convinced me that my first impression had been right. She had been topping up and nothing now could make her jump.

Nor did she notice much either.

As we began to walk off the steps I said, 'Did you think I was staying with you? I fixed otherwise.'

'Lucia said you would be back.'

'Ah yes, Lucia,' I said, peering into the overgrown gloom.

I couldn't see anything moving.

'Mustn't forget to lock up,' I said.

She did not even watch as I closed the door, hooked on the padlock and locked it with my 'key'. She stood there like a wax model, looking the other way.

'You wish for nothing?' she said, as I came away from the doors.

'No, thanks,' I said. 'Please tell Lucia I shall look in later. I would like some exercise.'

She bowed her head and walked off so smoothly she might have been sliding away on roller skates.

When she had gone there was a silence all round me. The sudden tearing shriek of a screech owl shook me as I stood there trying to make up my mind what to do.

My friend had tried to lock me in the vaults, meaning, perhaps, that I shouldn't get out alive. Perhaps he was the guardian of the treasure.

If so, was it Johnny?

It certainly wasn't a ghost. No ghost

could shove a coffin into my midriff with such force or sling a knife with such stirring accuracy.

Tracing back to Laura's story, Alaski had been forced down into the vault with a pistol in his back. Perhaps the shot she had heard was merely to convince Alaski the gun was loaded.

So he had been forced down there and shut in. He had stayed, going mad, for, say, twenty-four hours, then someone had got him out and hanged him from the chapel beam.

Well, he had risked coming back, and from what I knew he had well earned his fate. At any other period of Law he would have got that ending from a public hangman on his past record.

But he had come back wearing sneakers, so he had meant to be quiet. He had been caught, and now he was dead. All right, but where was I getting?

That treasure was enough to make men fight to the death. The keeper of it had waited for me, but had chosen to flee and fight another day. And it was some risk he had taken in fleeing. A false step would have seen the end of him.

Yet he had risked that rather than come down and let me see his face.

Then it must have been Johnny!

But how?

All done with mirrors. The illusion of reflection. Two men with the same face.

Fred the Nose had said she had come with 'the children '. He could have meant two, or three. But had there been twin boys, everyone in Dead End would have known.

And it appeared nobody knew. Everybody had known Johnny. That was all. Nobody knew any Johnny Two.

It was all very fascinating.

What was more attractive was that my Mini station wagon stood round the corner in the old stables, and a fortune in jewellery was lying there in the vault.

I went back and opened the vestry door.

It was easy, because the padlock had rusted almost through and a quick twist broke the remains of the hasp. I turned the solid iron handle and the door opened in. That smell from the vaults came out at me, but a ghost of its former aroma.

That was all right. My difficulty would be to get the car up here in comparative silence, and as it was a souped-up version of a common article one of the last things it possessed was a degree of quietness.

The stars were out. I could see quite well as I went round the chapel along the old paved path to the vestry. There was about six foot clear between the small trees and the high grasses where the tombstones leered.

The path curved round the corner of the stables and joined the house drive. I looked left along the stable fronts and there was my car, gleaming a little under the starlight.

My mind was made up, changed grasshopperwise.

I opened the door and put the brake off, then I pushed. She is easy to go, but rumbled a bit over the cobbles. I stopped at the corner and listened.

Something scuttered away at speed through the undergrowth, and it wasn't human.

I leaned against the front and started her backwards. Then I went alongside and steered through the window. There was a very slight fall towards the vestry, which helped.

Now and again a tyre grunched on some stones, but there was no point in stopping to listen any more. Speed and a gun in my pocket were the two essentials then.

I rolled her up close to the vestry door and stopped, opened the door and braked her there. Then I listened, just for new time's sake, but heard nothing. I opened the back doors and left them yawning on the stays. From the inside I snapped my three-cell flash from its spring catches, took my sample suitcase, emptied it and went into the vestry.

I got the chill again when I came into the low vault, but when the torch beam struck the jewels there was such a sparkling blaze of rainbow colour I felt quite warm again. I dug around into the glittering mass with my fingers. There was a lot of stuff there. It must have taken a collector years, or a thief. It was all saleable stuff, pearls, stones, necklaces, ear-rings, rings, no golden goblets or meltables at all that I could see.

I opened the suitcase—it was really a zip holdall type of bag, soft, and could swell. It started to swell now as I shovelled the goodies into it, almost blinded by the rivers of rainbow lights that hurried down through my fingers.

All the time I loaded I was conscious of my heart thudding. Often I stopped and listened, but heard nothing at all.

It was an extraordinary feeling, all that money bulging the bag out. I went on until I felt some kind of velvet cloth, and something underneath.

I shone the light in. The shallow layer of the jewels had almost been cleared by my hasty fingers.

I was not to look for any more, though scattered pieces still lay around on the velvet cloth, but to obey an instinct which I could never have left unsatisfied.

I went to the head of the coffin and pulled back the crumpled velvet.

The rich sunburn had gone, for the features had been doctored by the funeral specialists, but I recognised Johnny all right. It was both a shock and a relief to know that he was there, dead. So he *had* been returned.

I covered him up and put the lid back. Till then I had thought of the coffin as nothing more than a treasure chest. Now I felt rather like a grave robber.

I zipped the bag. It was heavy when I lifted it. I put it down a moment, then held the torch in the handles, which left me a free hand holding the pistol.

But nobody showed. As I passed through the vestry the edge of the light fell on Alaski's body, eyes open, watching me. It gave me the chills. I went out of the vestry door to the waiting car. Nothing moved but the thudding blood in my veins.

The bag was breaking my fingers. I pocketed the gun, snicked off the light and pushed the bag into the car. As I closed the doors I fully expected someone to come creeping out of the shadows, but nobody did.

Once more I put off the brake and trundled the car back down the lane between the lurching stones. Past the corner of the stables the drive fell towards the gates and the lodge. I let her roll and got in behind the wheel leaving the door open.

Out of the gates I started up and drove slowly along under the stars towards the village.

Lights were on at the inn windows. I drove slower, then turned round into the yard behind the building. When I switched off I didn't hear any noise of carousing. The citizens must have all gone home.

I got out, went round and got the heavy bag out of the back. Then I looked all round me. There was just me and the stars.

The yard door was open and I went in, watching myself approaching in the mirror. At the angle the light shone on the passage wall from the kitchen.

My shoes made no sound as I went towards it, and stood back so I could see in. Laura was standing there by the table, staring at nothing. She didn't know I was there.

'Pull the curtains,' I said and went in. As she hesitated in surprise, I said it again as if I would kick her, 'Pull the curtains!'

Then she did it and turned back to me

as I shut the door. I put the bag on the table.

'There you are, Laura,' I said. 'That's what you wanted.'

CHAPTER VII

I

She stood there a moment, looking at me, hands on her hips, challenging and beautiful. The light suited her rich Spanish looks.

'Well, go on,' I said, going to the door. 'It cost me a lot. Have a look, I'll get myself a beer.'

I went out into the empty bar. The central hanging oil lamp was on but turned low, glowing like Saturn in the murk of space. The chairs stood around untidily, like people suddenly stilled, watching me. I got my beer and drank a lot, then went back into the kitchen.

She had unzipped the bag and was standing there, just looking at it.

'Where did you find it?' She did not look up, mesmerised by the glories of wealth.

'In Johnny's coffin,' I said.

Then she did look up, eyes big, mouth slightly open in horror.

'No!' she hissed.

'Where did you think it would be?' I asked.

She recollected herself and looked away.

'I didn't know,' she said. 'But not there!'

'That's only because you're scared of thinking of such places,' I said.

Her mind drifted. She let her fingers dip into the bag and begin to lift the pearl strings and spill them back again. It was like watching little chains of rainbow fire.

'Well, that's yours,' I said. 'It was in his coffin, and you're his next-of-kin—his mother.'

She watched the moving lights of the jewels.

'Aren't you?' I said.

'Of course.' She looked up at me,

challenging again, and I felt she was lying.

I wasn't sure whether this was because I had already made up my mind she wasn't Johnny's mother, or because of her defiance. I'd got to know her well enough by then to know she always went defiant when she lied.

I drank some beer and sat down on the bench by the table, the bag between us.

'Well, are you pleased?' I said.

'Of course!'

'Then do something for me,' I said.

'Well—all right.' She was suspicious.

'Johnny has a brother,' I said.

She played with the jewels.

'Look, be open with me now,' I said. 'Because this brother has a hard claim on what you have there. He might also be cross with me for finding it for you. In such circumstances, I might get killed. So might you. After all, that's quite an attractive baggage you have there.'

I laughed. She stood there, showing her teeth at the jewels.

'All right,' I said, getting up with my empty glass. 'Think about it.' I went out and got another bottle of beer. It was close that night, and nerves made my throat dry. I went back. She had shut the bag. 'Well?'

For a while she said nothing, then she sat down on the end of the bench.

'I didn't know,' she said.

'You didn't know there was a twin?'

'I didn't know,' she repeated.

'So Johnny wasn't your son.'

'I had him from a baby,' she replied.

'Were you paid?'

'Yes. I hadn't got any money otherwise.'

'Then who was Johnny?'

She stared at me, as if trying to think of an answer.

'I don't know,' she said at last.

'Now, look,' I said. 'Johnny was dead and you collected him from the mortuary.'

'Yes. They asked about burying.'

'The authorities,' I said, watching her. 'Did you want him back?'

'I was fond of him somehow. I had had him all his life, all but a few weeks.'

'And you put him in a family vault—the family vault, where the other masters of Dead End lie, five generations past which add up, from what I saw, to two hundred years of Haughters—that is, of course, including Johnny's twenty years. A race of middle-aged progenitors, or getting on that way. Now what possessed you to bury him there? Wishes or orders?'

'He was a Haughter.'

'How long did you know that?'

'Not till he was dead.'

'And how did you know then?'

'The brother came!' She went suddenly stiff and clapped her hands to her cheeks, fingers covering her eyes. 'God! It was like a nightmare—a ghost!'

'And the brother gave the order for the burial?' I said.

She recovered.

'No. Me, I did. It was all proper. There was a coffin and the funeral men came in from the town.'

'But the brother didn't show himself.'

'No.'

'Why didn't you say anything about this brother?'

'He threatened me.'

'But surely, this brother was next-of-kin?'

'Is he? I thought it was me—his mother!'

'No, legally it would be a brother, unless there was a will leaving it to you.'

'The only will is leaving everything to Johnny.'

I remembered it had been Chang—I had been told—who was in office because of that will. That was the reason why the Chinese was in Dead End, sorting things out.

'Do you know what was in the will, by way of property or money?'

'It was the house and all the land round here. Worth a lot of money these days.

Land is expensive.'

'Nothing about money?'

'I never heard of any.'

'Weren't you left anything?'

She laughed.

'A farm up on the hills.' She pointed to the window.

'Haworth's farm?'

'Yes. It is one of the properties. In the will it says to his mother—' She laughed suddenly. 'Me!'

'But you were always known as his mother.'

'Yes, but I wasn't. If I was I'd have known about the twin.'

'Do you think you were legally stated as the mother in order to show there was no twin brother?'

'It could be that he is just a double—an accident,' she said.

'Nobody ever heard of this twin till after Johnny was dead?'

'Nobody did, no. Not even me. I should have thought I would have known, or guessed somehow. It was such a long time that I had him. He was like mine, almost—'

'Why not quite?'

Then suddenly her whole attitude changed as memory stirred another side of her.

'Because he was a foreign little bastard! He was cruel and greedy. He enjoyed hurting people. He stole to make them cry, but he didn't give it back. He was like that as a little boy and when he grew up he was worse. That's how I knew he would have something hidden away! I knew there would be something! I knew it! Because he stole from me, and from Linda and from everybody else. Because he made them pay for mistakes they made—pay in money, and if they hadn't got any, then in what they had got. He was a fine, double dyed bastard. That's what Johnny was!'

It was on my tongue to ask if his father had been like that, but I had the feeling she might not have known the father. All she seemed to be sure of was that Johnny had been 'a foreign bastard ' and I felt she meant that in its real sense, though she might not have been sure of it.

Another matter seemed more important.

'You had Johnny sent back here. There was a family coffin for him, and a place in the vault. You arranged with a regular firm of undertakers to bury him. Was there a service?'

'Yes. A vicar came over. It was in the chapel.'

'I thought you hadn't been inside there?'

'I haven't. I didn't go to the funeral. Nobody went.'

'Nobody?' I was shocked.

'There was just the four men from the undertakers' and the vicar. They came here for their money after.'

It was an extraordinary vision, the service in the chapel with a droning cleric speaking to nobody but four mutes, all as deaf to his words as the dead man in the coffin.

'The vicar said he had never had one like it, but he had not expected much in this place. This is part of his parish and long ago he used to come, but the people didn't want to see him, and in the end wouldn't talk to him, so he didn't come any more. He had some sherry and he was quite cheerful about it. I think he liked me.'

That wasn't surprising.

'So,' I said, 'who put the coffin down in the vaults?'

'The undertakers' men. There wasn't anybody else. It would have been left out.'

I had no idea Johnny's popularity had gone so deep.

'After that, somebody got into the vault, opened the coffin and deposited this weighty mass of decoration on top of Johnny then went. And I'd say nobody went there again till you saw Alaski being shoved down there.'

She shuddered.

'I don't want to remember that!' she said.

'I don't think you do remember it!' I said. 'Now, listen. You said he was shot in the back, fell over and was carried down the vault by the two men of Chang's.'

'Yes.' She shut her eyes as if she were seeing it over again.

'Well, I know for sure that Alaski was alive in the vault, and didn't die until tonight.'

She opened her eyes wide as they would go.

'Tonight? You mean he was alive?'

'Yes. Would it have made a difference if you had known?'

She hesitated.

'Yes, it would. I might have done something for him, then. But I thought he was dead!'

'Now you know he wasn't. Think back. What did you see that night?'

'I thought that was what I saw!'

'This whole place is full of mirrors,' I said. 'I keep on coming across things I think I see, but which I don't see. This is just another of those cases. You thought you saw something that didn't happen. What you did see meant something else.

'Who fired the gun?'

'The woman—Lucia.'

'She was behind Alaski?'

'Yes, she was behind—a yard perhaps. I couldn't say now.'

'Then where were Ferdi and Ali?'

'They were either side—of Alaski.'

'Close to? Holding him?'

She shut her eyes then opened them again.

'No, no. Spread out. Quite wide.'

'So that all four might have been searching the wood for something?'

She stared, then frowned.

'Well, could be. I never thought of that.'

'Then Lucia fired the gun.' I pointed across the room at right angles to her line of sight. 'Am I pointing at the bag?'

'Yes.'

'Well, I'm not. I'm pointing over at the

cupboard door. But the only thing you can see, linking my finger with your wish to close the circuit is that bag. I think you closed the circuit between Lucia's gun and Alaski. She could have fired at something else—something in the bushes.'

'I don't know!'

'Well, all right. Don't panic. Then Alaski fell down. How did he fall?'

'He grabbed his tummy and doubled up. I remember it very clearly, how he fell.'

'But if a man is shot in the back he isn't likely to clasp his middle, and usually he would be jerked forward by the kick in the back. The way you saw it seems to me to suggest that something you didn't see hit him in the tummy.'

'I don't know,' she said.

'When did you see this happen?'

'It was last night.'

I couldn't remember if that was what she'd said before. My memory swoops about, like my decisions, but in my situation I had decided to use memory alone, with its defects, rather than be found at some time with a bunch of incriminating notes that I couldn't lie a way out of.

'What were you doing up there?'

'I was having a look. You know why.'

'This was after you had shut the pub? What time?'

'Straight after. Eleven.'

'You saw it happen by the moon, you said.'

'Yes.'

'What time did you get back?'

'I came straight back. I wasn't going to hang about, after that. I was not gone half an hour.'

'Sure?'

'Dead sure, dead, dead!'

'The moon didn't come up till one last night,' I said. 'It's an old one and gets up late.'

'But I saw—!'

'Are you sure you saw Alaski?'

'He was in the middle.'

'Even in moonlight—what made you sure?'

'It was his way of walking. I couldn't be wrong.'

Laura, I knew, could always be wrong, and the wronger she was the harder she would swear she was right. But this time I felt she really thought she was right. But she, like me, was just a victim of another form of the old Chinese Boot Trick.

She had seen certain ingredients, such as people, and had been fooled into making a certain scene out of them.

She got up while I was staring at her, thinking.

'Take that bag away,' she said, fiercely. 'I don't want any of it!'

She swung away to the door.

'That's what I hoped you'd say,' I said, and got off the bench, tucking the heavy bag under my left arm.

I went out, through the bar with its Saturn glow hanging in the middle of dark nothing. She was at the end of the room. She may have been watching me, I don't know. She did nothing to stop me.

I went up the stairs to the corridor, then along it to Johnny's room. It was as I went in that I had the idea why she had acted like she had.

With the bag in my hands, Johnny's brother would come to me, and surely one of us would suffer. Or perhaps she knew he would come; perhaps she meant to tell him and make sure he'd come.

Perhaps I thought of that because it was in the back of my mind, too.

To my impatient brain it seemed a way to quicken things up, to stop off the tension with a direct confrontation.

I went back to the top of the stairs.

'What's his name? The brother.'

She turned her face up to me.

'No name I know.'

'I'll call him Nemo,' I said. 'That fits.' I leaned on the railing, letting the bag rest there so she could see it. 'Tell him I've got this.'

She stood like a statue.

'Aren't you afraid?' she said.

'So you know how to tell him?'

She pointed to the wall. For the first time I noticed an old fashioned speaking tube fixed there, a wooden whistle plugged in, the brass chain green.

'Where does it go?' I said.

She shrugged.

'You can't follow it. You just speak.'

True enough. You couldn't follow the route of such a tube without a builder or a demolition squad. It could go upstairs, downstairs, left, right, underground—to another cottage even. Judging from what little I knew of speaking tubes, I should say they stopped being part of household equipment seventy years ago, and whoever had put this one in was dead.

'You just speak?' I said.

'I just speak.'

'Is there an answer?'

'Yes, there is an answer,' she said and went to the bar. She went along the counter to a gaudy looking toy parrot standing at the end. She pulled a string out of its back, and as the string went back the bird nodded and said, 'It is a pretty morning. I love you. It is a pretty morning. I love—' then the grating voice lost speed and growled down to an unintelligible stop. 'One of these,' she said.

I had a chill crawling up my back. I have a horror of waxworks or things that ape human shape or voices. I leaned on the bag with my left elbow.

'Tell him, then,' I said.

She hesitated, then I saw her big dark eyes go from my face to the bag. Then she turned to the old speaking tube and pulled out the whistle. She blew. Nothing happened so far as I could hear.

'The man has Johnny's fortune,' she

said. 'The man upstairs.'

Nothing happened, and then I heard a faint squawking from the tube. She plunged the whistle back as if to stop the dreadful noise, then rubbed her hands down her thighs and looked up at me.

'Thanks,' I said, above the racket of my heart thudding in my ears.

She just looked.

As I walked slowly back along the dark passage I wondered how far that call had travelled. It could have been a long way off, or just downstairs in the cellar, or just in some other room, or even in the room I was heading for.

In the narrow passage my little light seemed bright and adequate for my eyes, but not for my fears. I knew I was a fool to be so impatient. Impatience, after all, was only a nervous state. To salve my jumps I had invited a fight now, when I was tired, when sense of any sort should have told me to hang on, lie quiet, get my breath back and have a couple of hours sleep.

Instead I roared on like a lunatic with his foot down in an Aston Martin and a wall blister on his front tyre. Crack soon, and swerve and away out of hand and the world would collapse all around.

Then I remembered I once had a burst in an Aston and she held it like a thoroughbred, fighting me, but playing the game all through. It made me feel better to remember.

My inferiority is a simplex.

Johnny's door was shut and I opened it carefully and quietly. As it swung I saw the sprinkling of bright stars through the opposite windows. They had a friendly look, I felt I could walk right through the bars and the glass and out along the invisible bridge of space up amongst them.

I wished I could.

There seemed one thing to do now. Pack the jewels and get out of Dead End, truly, for the last time. No return after this.

But Magog was still up there somewhere in that room.

I put the bag on the bed and watched the stars. I didn't know where Johnny's treasure had come from. It might he identifiable. Fond as I am of an ironic twist I did not care for the idea of doing a few years for having committed Johnny's theft.

Why wait, anyhow? What was the need to meet Nemo? What was the matter with me? I didn't have to stick now. I had money. I didn't have to finish the job. For me it was done.

But I didn't trust the contents of the bag. Everything that Johnny had done had turned out to be unlucky, for he had died over it. There was no special wish in me to do the same.

Yet, idiotically, I had to know.

The gun was still cold in my pocket, as if it refused to share my warmth.

There was a feeling in me that I was bent on self-destruction, as if some second

Jonathan Blake just shoved me on to disaster, and I stumbled forward, resisting but not strong enough to beat him back.

The stars laughed. I picked up the bag, turned and went quietly out into the passage again. I didn't use the torch this time but went towards the greenish glow of the big hanging lamp beyond the banisters.

When I got to the landing I looked down. The bar was empty. As I went down I eyed the snake's head of the old speaking tube, and had a crawly feeling it might suddenly shrill out and call someone to see my escape.

At the bottom there were two ways for me. One to unbolt the bar door and go out there, the other down the passage past the kitchen. The second was nearest to the car.

Some seconds ticked by while I stood by the counter, listening. I heard the busy clack of the old wooden kitchen clock she had on the mantel over the stove.

It travelled the distance from the kitchen bravely through the silence.

The counter flap was open. I went through and towards the passage door, which hung open against the wall. As I went into the passage I saw my reflection down the far end.

Someone had opened the mirror door again.

The reflection was not clear, for there was only the moonglow of the turned-down light behind me. There was just this odd sensation of hurrying towards myself.

Then I saw my reflection had no bag tucked under his arm.

Both his hands were hanging at his sides as he came towards me.

There was a moment of complete stillness in my body, all my muscles, all my vitals frozen with the horror of realisation.

The kitchen doorway was at my side. I stepped in. As I did it, I saw my 'reflection' halt. He had not seen me as soon as I had seen him.

I put the bag silently behind the door and got my gun out. Silence but for the ticking of the clock.

A smell of smoky paraffin drifted down the passage. The moonglow of the lamp faded, brightened, then died right out. Complete darkness fell.

My face froze with the burst of sweat on it. I tried to fix the doorway in my mind, keeping my eyes on where I remembered it had been. But my nerves were swinging. I began to doubt my memory. My thumb hesitated on the safety catch.

If I fired and hit the wall, I would show flame and my advantage would be gone, because I felt sure that Nemo had not come unprepared this time. The way he had slung that knife in the chapel told me he wouldn't need more than a gunflash to get his sights right for a throw.

With my left hand I felt the darkness and touched the edge of the open door. I touched the loose iron latch and it rattled. No movement followed the telltale noise.

But now I had located the door for sure, I knew my angle to reach the outer door across the room. Gingerly I felt down the door edge to the top of the bag, then crawled my fingers over the zip till I got the handle.

The pungent smell of the burnt out lamp irritated my nose. I felt I would sneeze and held my breath in sudden panic.

Still nothing happened in the passage. He thought he could outwait me, try a test of nerves. Did he know me that well to guess I wasn't the kind for the long, silent strain? If so, who in hell was he?

Slowly, step by step and being dead silent, I carried the bag backwards across the big kitchen. My heart jumped a bit in joy as I began to make out the grey square of the window I had made Laura curtain. The escape door was right beside it.

My progress was very slow, very cautious, I didn't want to hit the form or the table and make a giveaway grunt. The window became even clearer in the corner of my eye.

Then another emotion swamped my rising hopes.

It was not my eyes growing accustomed to the dark. There was a light approaching the window from outside.

It brightened suddenly as if it had just rounded an outjutting corner of the building. The sudden glare was dazzling. Anyone at the passage door must see me if his line of sight was right.

I ducked and fled in behind the outer door. The handle rattled, then the door came open, covering me against the wall.

The light was brilliant. Somebody carried it in and stood it on the table, a flaring electric lantern covering the passage door, blazing on the empty wall beyond.

Laura moved round the table, half silhouette, half blazing overdeveloped light where the edge of the beam caught her.

She stopped, staring towards the passage

doorway. She could see something I could not.

'What the hell are you doing there?' she said.

There was no answer, but there must have been a sign, for she looked round the kitchen nervously, quickly.

I was behind an open yard door. I might get round it and out, but it would have to be quick. Yet once in the starlit yard, I felt I could handle the situation. So long as we could see each other, the chances were fair.

Again my sense of irony was spiked when I realised I had run into a man I had decided not to wait for, and feared him the more now because I had been fool enough to call him myself.

Laura stood still by the table. Clearly she obeyed some sign instruction from the unseen man in the passage. That didn't surprise me, that she obeyed him. He had the hold of fear on her. She had lied when she had told me he hadn't been in the bedroom for the same fearful reason that she stayed still now.

Then she started to give.

'There is no one,' she said, terrified. 'What—'

Again she was silenced, and there must have been more signs.

She leant over the table and turned the lantern away from the passage door slowly, watching the doorway as if for directions. The broad flood of light passed over the yard door, covered me with black shadow from the door as deep as mourning black, then went on round the room, slowly, like a small lighthouse.

When it came to the passage door again, I saw her tense, then keep the lamp turning. She turned it until once more the flood covered the yard doorway and flanked my funeral shadow with revealing light either side.

She watched the door, then turned towards me. She hesitated, and I saw her take a deep breath, then reluctantly she came towards me. To me her coming was like a scene in slow motion. I could count every tiny movement she made.

Then she stopped, her hands on her hips and looked behind the door.

She could see me then, though no more than a huddled grey shadow clutching the bag.

She came closer and touched the edge of the door. The smell of the paraffin was fleeing out of the open door, and now I could smell her scent.

We looked at each other, and then she turned slightly.

'There's nothing here,' she said.

For a moment she did not look back towards the passage, scared of her lie, but then she knew she would have to, and she did.

I knew what the next signal would be. She would be told to close the door so he could see behind it.

Once more she turned back towards me. Once more she was within touching distance, my gun pointed dead at her as she stood silhouetted slightly to the left of the light.

Her hand came out and gripped the edge of the door.

In the backglare I saw her face and I knew she didn't want to close that door.

In the dragging seconds I could see the battle in her, and I kept hoping she would decide in my favour.

But she couldn't.

Her fear of Nemo was now the greater driving force in her life.

Her hand tightened on the edge of the door.

It began to swing, letting the flood of light crawl across the wall towards me.

I thumbed up the safety catch.

I fired.

CHAPTER VIII

I

It was a good shot, and good for me it was. It got the light right in the lens and blacked it out. I slipped the gun into my pocket, grabbed Laura by the arm and dragged her round the door and out into the starlight.

'Get in the car,' I said. 'Can you drive?'

She gasped.

'Yes.'

'Get in and drive. I'll do the shooting.'

I covered the open door. She ran round and got in my car. I backed against it, opened the door and slung the bag inside. The whole thing took a few seconds. The man hadn't come out by the time I had my gun ready.

The car was between me and the open door and I was going to shoot over the roof. I reckoned he would not have much of a knife-shot with just my head for a target.

It must have been a good tableau we presented when the car appeared round the ramshackle cottages and headed towards us. It had only sidelights on or we would have seen it before.

I slipped the gun into my pocket quick. Laura squeaked something and scrambled out of the car.

The big, black car stopped, looking dead at us with dark eyes. A man got out and I saw his buttons glittering in the starlight.

The police patrol had arrived. What a splendid time for them, with a bagful of swag in the car and an unlicensed gun in my pocket, a dead man up at the chapel with my prints all over the locks and the book and the candlesticks and the pews! Tally-ho, policeman! The fox is bagged.

He was an inspector, and he smiled at

Laura. Laura didn't seem to know what to do, but after a moment of flustering, she became cheerful and gay.

'Hallo, Inspector, dear,' she said. 'You're very late tonight.'

'Pressure of business,' smiled the Inspector, looking towards me. 'All well, Laura?'

'Yes, thank you,' she smiled at him.

'A visitor,' said the Inspector, still watching me.

'The season isn't over, then.'

'This is Mr. Blake, he is staying a few days,' Laura said.

'Business trip,' I said. 'I'm a rep.'

'I thought you said rip!' The Inspector laughed. He was easily amused. He turned back to Laura. 'Chinaman still up at the Manor?'

'Yes.'

'Fu Manchu in person,' said the Inspector. 'Isn't he some sort of a solicitor?'

'He's doing the estate,' said Laura.

'By the way, a man called at the station

a couple of days back asking where Johnny was buried,' the Inspector said. 'Did he come here?'

'What kind of a man?'

I could sense a sharp, frightened edge to Laura's voice.

'Young chap. Very fair. Seemed to think Johnny might be in a pauper's grave, or at least an official one. Still, if he didn't come perhaps you can look forward to him.'

He said goodnight and went slowly back to the car. He seemed to be doubting whether to go, but in the end he got in, and the engine started. The car swung round and went slowly away.

'Is that all he usually does?' I said.

'It is not usually him, but a sergeant.'

We both looked back to the open door.

'What are you going to do?' she whispered urgently.

'I don't want to run up behind them.' I shook my head towards the slowly retreating car.

'Then what?'

I opened the back door, got my long distance flash and the bag out.

'I'm going to find him,' I said. 'You hang on here.'

'No! He might get me. I'll come behind you.'

'Why should he get you?' I wasn't thinking very hard.

'I hid you behind that door when he told me to look,' she said.

Suddenly I felt a great wave of hot, grateful love for Laura. I even let the open door go hang and kissed her so that she wriggled against me. Then she pushed me away, breathless, and shook her head.

'You take silly risks—' She hissed the words. 'He might be behind you!'

I snatched the beam torch off the car roof and shone it into the doorway. It was empty.

'What does he look like?—truthfully now.'

She shook her head.

'I don't know.'

'But you saw him—in the bedroom—when he was signalling to you just now—'

'He makes up all the time. I can't see what he looks like.'

'Disguise, do you mean?'

'It's that makes him look like Johnny. He does it to make himself look like it. But it's make-up, you can see.'

'So he could be the man with the yellow hair at the police station?'

'He could be anybody.'

'We'll find for sure.'

Out of respect to him we had spoken very low and I had watched the building all the time. I began to get the feeling the place was empty, that Nemo had gone when the police came.

He hadn't been afraid to call on them a couple of days ago, but since then Alaski had died. Perhaps that explained Nemo's change of attitude to the polizei.

I went towards the building, and she came close behind, a good rearguard.

There wasn't much point in overcaution

with the blazing light in my left hand, bag under that arm, and the gun, catch up, in my right. We went quickly and quietly through the kitchen, the magic mirror passage and the bar. All empty, places of shadows massing round the light beam.

The other ground floor rooms were empty. My feeling that he had gone grew stronger with each step we took, but I didn't let this make me easy.

We went up the stairs. She held the back of the waistband of my trousers as if not to let me get away from her going up.

The passage was empty. We went along, room to room, shoving the doors open, shining the torch round, the gun ready beside it.

Nothing.

We came to Johnny's room. The range of door-knockers flared brassily back at the light, explosions of brilliance in the darkness.

'I must do the attic alone,' I said. 'You stay in here.'

'Be quick!' she whispered.

'Quick as paint,' I said and shut her in with the bag.

I did not use the light now, for I had the ladder to get up. I stood a minute to get my eyes working smoothly by the faint light, then went up the ladder carefully, and quietly.

When my head and shoulders were through the trap I held the gun ready, switched on the light and swung it round like a radar scanner. Rubbish, stacks of it, shadow and whirling dust, but no hiding man.

I went up on to the floor and went quickly the length of the place, shining the light into every alcove, behind every stack of junk. The place was empty of men but me.

At the bottom of the ladder I flashed the light down the corridor again, and it was empty as before.

I tapped on Johnny's door, opened it and went in. She had been waiting for me. At the very instant I slipped the gun back in my pocket she grabbed my other wrist.

'Put it out!' she hissed.

I did. Then she came against me, her breasts moving against my chest and she found my lips in the dark. Her arms stole round my neck, and as I had always felt the sensual urge about her, I let go and joined in. She got hot. I hadn't had such a kiss in months, nor the feeling of splendid, voluptuous abandon enveloping me.

'Come on, come on, Johnny Blake,' she whispered. 'He has gone. There is nothing—till tomorrow. He won't come again now.'

We moved away from the door together, each as urgent as the other and my weakness for her and love in general let me persuade myself it was time to make a break. We stumbled against the bed and fell on it, laughing in the darkness.

I forgot the gun was in the pocket of my trousers.

Making love with Laura is rather like wrestling with a playful and passionate bear. The gun kept digging into my thigh and hers. I took it out of the pocket and fumbled it on to a table.

Soon after that I had the sudden feeling someone else was in the room with us. I held her still and put a hand over her mouth. The bed creaked as she struggled and I couldn't hear properly.

There was a shadow against the wall, where the starlight just caught the golden faces of the door-knockers. It was someone close by the table where I had put the gun.

I let her go suddenly and snatched for the gun. She clung to me.

'No, no! Don't! He'll kill you!' she gasped.

I got a hold on the gun. So did he. I pulled back like hell and saw him half twist, but as I broke his hold he got another, on my wrist.

Struggling on a bed with a desperate woman holding my left arm and a more desperate man holding my right and trying to tear my gun away from me is one pastime I don't want again.

You can't win.

He hit me on the head with his fist and it flashed in my eyes like fireworks, but I managed to hold on to the gun somehow. He tore and pulled and hit me again. I felt I was going down through water, clinging to the gun as the last straw and bearing a struggling woman round my neck, more scared of drowning than I was.

There was a crack and the flash was blinding. The grip on me didn't give at once, but eased off slowly. I saw the man move back across the window, his head turned upwards. Then he began to sink down. There was a thud just after he cleared the window, and then a groan, and then nothing.

Laura was still stiff, holding her breath.

'My God!' she exploded.

'Let go,' I said.

She did. I got up, swaying about. Things were still not fixed in my eyes after the head whacks, and I did not fully believe what I had seen, though some kind of natural dread sickened me with truth.

I fumbled around and found the torch. She was huddled on the bed, breathing so fast it was like sobbing.

The man was still on the floor by the foot of the bed.

'Is he dead?' she hissed.

I wiped my wet face with the flat of my hand and kept looking.

'Twice,' I croaked at her. 'This is the second time!'

The man was Alaski, dead once already by hanging.

2

When you keep seeing something you know

damned well isn't there you can begin to get frightened of your head. I was dead scared of mine then. The Chinese Boot Trick was becoming terrifying. Double men, double faces, double identities, all bloody doubles. You couldn't tell if you were looking at the real or the reflection.

You were inclined to defend yourself against the wrong one.

Laura got off the bed, pulling her clothes together.

For me the shock cleared slowly like smoke from an explosion. Then I looked at the dead man again. He did look like Alaski, very much like him, but he was a great deal younger when you looked into it. But if you took another angle of the still face you could see it was like Johnny too.

Of course. Alaski the father of the two boys. Not twins, but Nemo shared the looks of both.

The explanation made me feel better. I could have seen this face, made up, as

Laura had said, down through the trap and it could have looked exactly like Johnny.

Just as a minute before, the first sight of the new-dead face had looked like Alaski, for the man looked more like the politician than like his brother.

'That's him—that's the man,' she whispered. 'Is he dead?'

'Yes.'

The gun was lying on the floor. In the course of the confusion I didn't even know if I had pulled the trigger or he had. It didn't much matter. I stowed the gun in my pocket once more.

'What are you going to do?' she whispered hoarsely.

'A good question,' I said. 'I'm damned if I can answer it.'

'It's lucky the police came first,' she said, getting her voice back. 'You'll have time.'

'Time for what?' I said.

'You can't leave him here!' She shuddered suddenly.

'No,' I said. 'I've got to think. Get me a drink, Laura. I think better alone.'

She went out. I sat on the bed and thought about the mess everything was in. There was Alaski dead in the chapel, his son dead at my feet. Only me left for anyone to blame, so it would seem to anyone with a depression on.

It didn't seem worth while to go over any excuses I might put forward at a trial. I had come here to find stolen property, and I'd certainly found some I hadn't expected and two men were dead. You might say they had killed themselves, one way and the other.

The law usually likes to have something neat, ends tied in. The only way I could see it could tie up neatly was to use me.

Laura came back with a drink and I was grateful. My throat was like hot sand.

'You've got to take him to the vault. It's the only place,' she said, rubbing her thighs with her palms. She always did that when excited.

241

The idea was the correct one.

'All right,' I said. 'I'll decide for certain later. The only thing is, you keep out of it. Whatever might be found afterwards will be my affair.'

She nodded, then swallowed.

'Yes,' she said.

I drank the beer. My feelings then were to give up and flop. I felt it couldn't be worth the tension of going on, of trying to fight my way out of a cell of adverse circumstance.

But it had to be done.

When the dryness went from my throat I felt better, my head clearer. I looked at her, pale and somehow wonderful in the starlight.

'Did you know he was in here with us?' I said.

'I knew he would come,' she said. 'There is a door in this wall somewhere. I know Johnny used it when he didn't want to be seen.'

'So you tried to save me a second time,

Laura. This is getting monotonous. What did you hope would happen?'

'You would fall asleep and he would take the bag and go.'

'He didn't try for the bag, he tried for the gun.'

'Because you heard him. You shouldn't have. I wasn't good enough.' She shook her head.

'You were all right,' I said. 'It was just I was too scared to concentrate. Where's this opening?'

'I don't know. Don't waste time looking. Use your car.'

'He should have left it ready to nip back into,' I said, and used the light again to switch round the room.

The door-knockers beamed back. I realised then that they could have been not so much a collection as a wall disguise.

'Don't waste time!' she urged.

'It might be a better hiding place,' I said. 'Hang on a minute.'

'But—'

She stopped short and I stood where I was. Someone was knocking on a door downstairs, a quick, sure sound of somebody who knew they must be let in.

'Who's that?' I said, without realising the stupidity of the question.

'I don't know,' she said, desperately. 'Perhaps the police came back!'

'Well, go and talk to 'em,' I said. 'Say I've gone to bed.'

Her hair was down to her shoulders. She ran off and I saw her go down the passage into her room. The moon was coming up, for the light was stronger. She came out of the room again, slipping a dressing-gown over her shoulders.

The knocking came again.

Fear crawled like worms over my skin. If it was the police, why in hell had they come back?

Memory showed them going away slowly, as if in doubt about something. Suspicion showed them halting up the winding exit to Dead End, then coming back to surprise.

I looked round the walls again. Nemo had seemed to come from behind me, and I had a good look there. It was the wall by the door.

Below I heard voices, but they were indistinct and I hadn't time to bother with them. My business was to get dead Nemo out of the bedroom before they came up.

Then, by some trick of acoustics the voices became suddenly clear.

'We just had a call to come back here. Message said a man was shot dead.'

I recognised the Inspector's voice.

'Shot dead? No! There's a mistake. How on earth did you get such a message?'

Laura was on the ball. It was strange how she faced up to shocks with a sharper brain than she normally used.

'Somebody phoned. We got the wireless,' said the Inspector.

'But you know I haven't got a phone!'

'Where is one, then?'

'The Manor is the only one.'

'Funny. They said the call came from

here. Stevens, go out and call HQ. Get them to verify.'

'It must be a hoax,' I heard Laura say.

I couldn't find any crack in the wall, a necessity for me now, as there was no other way out of the place. The Inspector was in the bar downstairs.

'This isn't the sort of place I'd suspect hoaxers to be,' said the Inspector. 'Got it, Stevens?'

'Smart work,' said Stevens, short of breath. 'There is no phone in Dead End now. The Manor one was cut off two months back.'

'I told you!' Laura cried out in triumph.

'Well, that's queer,' the Inspector said. 'It said here, in the end room, first floor. Very direct, it was.'

I had the instinct then that he was going to come up and look, just to satisfy everybody.

'But there's somebody asleep there—a guest,' said Laura, very loudly.

'All the same, it's so queer I'd like to

look, Laura,' the Inspector said.

I shut the door. Then I went round the bed and shoved Nemo, under it. Then I got into it. Then I waited, listening to my heartbeats.

Laura was protesting, I felt for sure, about her guest being interrupted in his sleep. It's just what she would do, but I could hear nothing through that soundproof door.

Then there came a knocking, full and half smothered by the padding. I did nothing. After a while it came again.

'What is it?' I bawled.

The door opened a little.

'The police are here,' Laura said.

'Well, I don't want them,' I grumbled. 'Tell 'em to come back in the morning.'

The door opened wider. I saw the Inspector's silver glinting in the grey light. A light flashed on towards me.

'Turn that damn thing away!' I shouted. 'What's the matter with you? This is the last time I sleep in this dead-and-alive hole!

I've got work to do tomorrow. Now get out and let me sleep.'

'Sorry to disturb you, sir. Goodnight.'

The door almost shut, then opened again. My heart stopped altogether. What had the sweep of that light shown as it had been withdrawn behind the closing door?

'Door-knockers,' said the Inspector. 'Thousands of 'em.'

The door shut. I lay back on the pillows a moment, really wishing I was in a position to drop off to sleep; real, guiltfree, dreamless sleep. It was the sort of thing I kept wishing because I was tiring rapidly now. I'd had enough, but my nerves wouldn't let me ease off and rest awhile. The very fact I kept wishing it made me more frightened to do it.

I stared at the wall where I had searched.

Door-knockers.

Well, if there was an opening there, a door-knocker would be a good disguise for a handle.

I hauled out of bed and began tugging

the line of knockers about the height of a highish door-handle. One pulled towards me and a hidden door opened.

My torch showed a quite wide passage behind and a normal flight of wooden stairs going down. What Johnny had done to make the little silent room—apparently next door—had been to block off an old staircase and make the little room out of the landing. Thus he had had a prison room and a private staircase down.

I pushed the door to, then went to the main door and opened it to listen. Laura came in, breathless and anxious. She looked very scared.

'You got rid of them?' I said.

'How did they know?' she gasped.

'Somebody saw,' I said. 'I found the door in the wall here. Somebody must have followed him and seen it.'

'But how did he telephone?'

'Plugged in to the overhead line somewhere,' I said. 'It's been done before. Neat, too. It nearly got us trapped up while they got on with the business ... I've got to get rid of Nemo.'

She shuddered.

'I'll help you,' she said.

'I'll be all right,' I said. 'You just shut the door after me.' I switched on the light. 'No, you'd better hold this.'

The light swept the room as I went to hand it to her. I swept by the empty table where earlier I had put the hold-all.

'The bag!' she said at once. 'It's gone!'

'Hardly surprising,' I said. 'Take hold.'

She took the light.

'I'm glad it's gone,' she said.

I stopped, half bent to reach under the bed.

'Why?' I said.

'I was frightened of it,' she said.

'You're barmy,' I said, and hauled the dead man out on to the carpet.

She watched while I humped him, firemanlike, then came behind me, shining the light past me. We went down the stairs.

'There's blood on your shirt,' she said.

'I've got some more back there—shirts, not blood.' I was grunting a bit by then. Humping a full size man is heavy work.

We went on down another flight. A door had been built up at the bottom of the first. Thus we came down into a cellar. I let Nemo rest on the stairs a bit and did some deep breathing. She shone the light round.

'It's part of the old cellar,' she said. 'But that—' she held the light on the entrance to a long passage, lined with breeze blocks, '—that's new.'

'It goes a long way,' I said. 'Who dug that out?'

'Must have been when they were tunnelling in the old quarry shafts,' she said. 'They tunnelled a long way then.'

'Then they did this while nobody was looking, just for Johnny,' I said. 'Let's go.'

Nemo seemed a bit lighter after the rest. We went into the tunnel. The floor was rough, just as it had been dug. Several times I stumbled on it. Whether it curved slowly or not I don't know. The torch beam just fizzled in the distance ahead.

After a while I rested again.

'It must go to the house,' she said.

'Or into the mine galleries,' I said, breathing hard. We went on. There was a crank in the tunnel, as if passing some downthrough obstruction, perhaps the corner of a cellar. As we turned the angle the light showed a wooden door ahead.

'We'll know now, anyhow,' I gasped and put Nemo down.

The door was easy, a sliding bolt. I shot it and opened the door, signalling her to put the light out. It was good I did, because there was a dim light beyond the door.

I was looking out of an alcove in one of the house cellars, and the light shone from a passage on the far side of the big, low room.

Someone was going away down the passage, carrying my bag. It could have been a tall, blond boy, with tight jeans, but I knew it wasn't.

As I looked the carrier's head turned and Lucia looked back over her shoulder.

Seeing her going away with the spoils tied up, I didn't wonder why she had taken so long to get here ahead of us, but just accepted the time lapse.

I didn't see how she could see me, but it seemed she did.

Suddenly, she dropped the bag on the passage floor and ran away out of sight round a corner in the corridor.

'She left the bag!' Laura hissed over my shoulder.

'Well, that's handy, isn't it?' I said, going out into the cellar.

'Don't touch it!' she whispered urgently. 'It's bad luck, I know!'

'You're just nervous,' I said.

Well, she had enough reason, too, considering what had happened since I had brought the damned bag back to the inn. I felt a little of her anxiety myself, but my superstition can be overruled by my greed.

Humping Nemo around had exhausted my patience more than anything else. I decided to ditch Magog and Lucia and the rest of them and risk them chasing me up in the future. I decided to take the bag and go, and take Laura with me. She had been a good ally, and I felt strongly that I didn't want to do without her any more.

'Hang on there,' I said.

'What are you going to do?' she said.

'Get the bag, leave that geezer in the tunnel and beat it with you. That's good enough, isn't it?'

'Don't take the bag! It won't do any good. It killed Johnny and Alaski and this man—there's a curse on it!'

'That's a relic of your gipsy upbringing,' I said. 'Things don't have curses, not if they're worth plenty of cash.'

I held up my hand to stop her talking. Then we listened. Lucia had gone, with whatever noise she was making. The place was quiet.

'Don't!' She clung on my arm, tightly.

'What else can we do?'

'Just go!'

It was then I realised that she probably loved me. Only a woman in love could be so daft as to suggest going with nothing but ourselves to live on.

'If you leave it, there's nothing they can want from you,' she said urgently. 'They'll leave you alone, don't you see?'

'But I haven't got money!' I lied. 'I'm a bandit. I depend on what I can pick up, and there's a fortune standing over there!'

'If you take it, then they'll come after you. There'll be no peace. They'll come after you and they'll—' she drew a deep, sharp breath, '—they'll kill you!'

'Well, they haven't yet, and they've tried,' I said.

'Kick out of it, Laura. We can take this risk together.'

'No!'

She clung on to my arm desperately, trying to pull me back towards the tunnel. She was strong and she could fight, and there were feelings inside me that held me back from hurting her.

'Let go!' I said.

I tried to tear her fingers off, but she started kicking.

'It's no good—just let's go! Please! Please just let's go!'

I shoved her against the cellar wall, got one hand free of my arm and then the other. She pressed back against the wall, panting, her eyes wild.

I turned to run for the passage. She must have thrown herself at my waist, rugby fashion, or perhaps it was a last desperate attempt to stop me by throwing herself bodily, just clawing out to catch some part of me.

She got my left leg, and I went down.

It was as I was falling that the bag blew up with a flash that seared my eyeballs and destroyed all vision.

CHAPTER IX

I

Sometimes the brain is blasted into activity. Or perhaps the flash of death speeds up the imagination, as to the drowning man.

As I went face down to the floor and liquid fire seemed to flash all round me, I realised that—if I wasn't dead already-Lucia and the others might reasonably think I was.

It was sheer accident on Laura's part that we were both flat on the ground when the explosion passed over. Had we been standing we should have had it. Even lying flat the tearing hot fingers of the expanding fire could be felt clawing my back. Dim in the heart of the deafening roar I heard Laura's thin scream.

The whole eruption seemed a long time dying. The roaring seemed to go on for minutes, but gradually I made out that this had changed from the tearing roar of explosion to the tumble and slither of some part of the wrecked building. The air was choking thick with dust.

In the end there was just darkness, the hot, pressing, gritty air and dazed fumbling in the dark as I got to my knees. I felt her clutching for me.

'Are you all right? Are you all right!' She gabbled desperately.

'I think so. Where are you?' I felt around and touched her head. 'Best find the torch—'

We scrabbled around the floor, digging amidst broken bits of plaster and dust. She found it, gave a little cry and switched on. It made it better. She kept saying 'Thank God ' and crying a bit. I rocked her in my arms as I squatted. We were both rattled, like frightened kids. I could hear the flashing thunder of the disaster over and over again rubbing in my nerves like a river bore in queer waves of fear.

'It was the wrong bag,' I tried to joke, but she clung tighter as if my humour made things worse.

After a while things cooled and we got up and looked around. Where the passage was there were just heaps of rubble. It looked as if it had rushed at us out of the passage mouth, like lava, for it reached the ceiling, which, above our bit, had lost plaster and patches of laths looked down like dirty, broken teeth. We looked at the muck in awe.

'Thanks for pulling me down,' I said, taking a deep breath.

I could almost feel myself standing there and being flung backwards through the air and smashed against the wall behind me.

She looked round to the door we had come in by. It was almost covered by some fallen beams which seemed to have given way when a brick buttress had crumbled. I saw now that the buttress, about eight feet across and three deep, was hollow. A bricked-in fireplace.

'The door!' she said. 'Can we get out?'

'We can shove that lot aside—if we're careful,' I said, watching the fireplace.

'Let's go then,' she said urgently. 'I can't bear it any longer. Let's get out of this place—right away!'

I still watched the old fireplace.

'Listen to me!' she said, shaking my arm.

'I heard you,' I said. 'We'll go but there's one thing I have to do before we go.'

I went towards the fireplace and some rubble and soot and muck which had fallen from the flues above. In the middle of the mess there was an odd, bright splash of jazzy colour.

'What is it?' she said, alarmed again. 'What are you looking at?'

'A horror comic,' I said.

'You're mad!' she hissed. 'Quickly! Let's go. They might come to find us—'

'There's only Lucia,' I said. 'She won't dig this lot to find us. Mrs. Chang is doped somewhere, probably wandering in the nude. She does that. I think she has something on her mind. Chang, possibly.'

'He might come back!' Laura said. 'You can't trust what that Lucia says. She just tried to kill you, didn't she?'

'She won't hang around,' I said going to the fireplace. 'You seem to forget, she's got the loot. She won't stick around with that. Only a fool would. I wish I hadn't.'

'Then come now!'

'The thing's different,' I said. 'You know what?' The flue goes right up to the room where I want most to go.'

'Oh no, no, no!'

'It won't take a few minutes,' I said, shaking her off my arm. 'I must!'

'You're a bloody minded clot!' she shouted, losing her temper. 'You'll kill yourself for being stupid!'

It wasn't any profit arguing with Laura.

'Hang on here,' I said ducking into the

fireplace with the torch in my hand.

'Hang on, hang on!' she cried. 'Damn, I won't! And in the dark! Not on your life! Damn you and hanging on all the time! Stop hanging on and go with me!'

I shone the beam up the flue. It was big, an old one, I'd say built before the 'modern' house, two hundred years before. There were old, withered iron rungs still standing out of the flue sides.

'It's a gift,' I said. 'Come in and hold the torch.'

'For God's sake, what are you going to do?' she demanded.

'Find an absent god,' I said. 'Hold the light.'

'I shall go with it!'

'I'll trust you.'

I dragged her down and under the lintel then gave her the light. She went to hit me with it, but I caught her in time.

'We can't afford that kind of dance,' I said. 'Cut it out and do as I say. Give me five minutes, and then I promise we'll go for good.'

'Promise?'

'Dead true, wet and dry, umbilical tie. Just keep it steady.'

I started to go up the lighted flue. Perhaps I was dizzy but suddenly it seemed I was climbing head first down a square well. I stopped, gripping the rungs hard. The light under me, the dazzling bright spot, added to the confusion. One moment I was climbing head down, then crawling along a level shaft, then scrambling upwards out of the vertical, tipping over backwards. I was beginning to go round like a giant Catherine wheel with the axis through my navel.

The reason was clear, but I tried not to see it. I had come back to Dead End too soon, insufficiently recovered, and what I had put my unfortunate frame through these last hours was just too much. I couldn't control the dizziness. It was getting worse.

The shaft began to swing wildly, I was plunging one moment, then reaching up and tipping over backwards the next. 'Cut the light a minute!' I whispered.

She snapped it out. In the blessed darkness I was lost, floating in space for a minute, and then began to steady.

'Okay,' I said. 'Let's have it again.'

She shone the light. I went on up. There was hardly any soot. No fires had been lit for years. Way up on top of me I saw the chimney partly blocked by the hefty twigs of a jackdaw's nest, left there, probably, year after year for new broods.

The ground floor flue opening went by. Only a few feet now to the hiding place of Magog, cause of all the trouble.

Then I heard the voice.

For a moment I thought it might be Laura, but the sound was coming from above me.

'Give it to me.' There was a pause. 'Put it on the desk there.' Pause. 'Thank you.'

It was Madame Chang, not doped this

time, judging from the sound of it.

'You can't get away with this.' Lucia sounded cold and unemotional, but I could hear the tension in her voice.

'You will see that I can,' the Chinese woman answered. 'It is what he came for.'

'Then why has he gone to London?'

'He has to play his part, the agent. It is necessary to show the right face in England.'

'You propose to go now? How?'

'I shall go.'

'Won't I follow?'

'You should not meddle with explosives. There are sticks left.'

This cold-blooded threat to dispose of Lucia by another explosion made me shiver as I clung there. Lucia had made the bomb from stock she had found left from the old blasting gangs in the quarry. She had invented the idea, now she was going to get it back.

Madame Chang was an even better

example of the old Chinese Boot Trick than I had even suspected. Her two faces had been superb. She had seemed blank, drugged, blandly stupid. Her coming nude into my room had all been a part of the act, nothing spared for verisimilitude.

And behind that even, soporific mask the cold, ticking brain had been working away like a little clock, moving on, unaffected by plot or threat. Now it had arrived at the conclusion.

She had let the others find the treasure. Now all she had to do was take it. Obviously she was holding Lucia up, and equally obviously she was going to keep her hold.

Then I heard the sound of Madame laughing. It was a strange sound, one I had never expected to hear.

'Take these,' said Madame, and there was an iron clank.

'Handcuffs!' Lucia said.

'If you do as I say, perhaps we will not have more bangs,' said Madame. 'Clip one over your wrist and make it lock. Now!' I heard the click, the flue acoustics were so good towards me. 'Good. Now go to the fireplace. You see the iron is moulded so there is a loop. Put the other cuff through the loop.'

'The hell with you—' Lucia began.

'It will be in hell with you if you do not do as I say,' Madame said, icily smooth. 'Kneel down. It will be better.'

I heard the iron scrabble and clank.

'That is right,' said Madame. 'Now clip the other on your wrist.' There was a pause, then a click that rang through the ironwork of the fireplace. 'Good. I will just make sure. Yes, that is very good. There is no key.'

There was a confused sound of movement, then a door shut. I heard Lucia breathing hard, muttering something in Greek. I guessed it had to do with unworthy women and such.

It had been a game of leapfrog, passing the bag. Now Madame had got the loot and having heard her I did not think anyone would make a final leap over her back.

But now Lucia was chained to the fireplace I had to get through.

As I clung there with my back resting against the other wall of the flue, I thought painfully that it was time the luck changed in my favour.

There was a sudden clanking and crunching as Lucia struggled in anger with the handcuffs.

Some bird, resting high above me, fluttered in alarm and plastered its departing gift on my forearm. It must have missed the jackdaw's nest by a miraculous fraction.

Such were my nerves then that I jerked hard on the rung, starting and not realising what it was that hit me. The rung came away with a queer little shifting noise and I was left, with my foot on a cramp below and my back pressing hard against the bricks to keep my position by friction.

My mother, when I was very young, said jokingly it was lucky to be dropped on by a bird. Suddenly I knew she was right.

For the rung had come clean out with a false brick and in the opening I saw something glow. It was a hard squarish glow; a metal box. I had seen before. It was Magog's tomb.

Oh blessed birdie! He had hidden there even in the face of my faint scrabblings, perhaps ready to go, but knowing I was too far away. But the metallic grinding of the handcuffs had really tuned in to his nerve. Oh, lucky, timid birdie with such a lovely nerve frequency!

I took out the box, hardly bigger than a brick but very heavy, and shoved back the false cover. Then I went slowly down again.

'What happened?' Laura said.

'I got the bird,' I said, whispering. I grabbed her arm and we ducked out of the fireplace. 'Easy. Someone up there can hear.'

We went towards the tunnel opening.

'You're going?' she said, startled.

'Yes. I've got what we need.'

When we got through the opening I saw the tunnel we had used had fallen in.

'Modern workmanship,' I said.

But it had buried Nemo.

2

We were left with the other way, the extension of the tunnel. There was no other way except up through the fireplaces and that would deal a hand to poor, trapped Lucia.

Laura pointed the torch. The tunnel cranked away. As we followed it, we kept on cranking. It must have been working its way round the footings and foundations of the old house.

Then suddenly the lining of breeze blocks ended. The floor sloped up and the walls were just rough hewn from the clay.

I saw a moving spot of light ahead and slightly above us.

'Snap that off!' I whispered.

She turned the torch off. We stared at the moving patch of light and then I let my breath go.

'The moon,' I said, relieved. 'Shining between leaves.'

'I thought it was somebody—' she hissed.

I pushed up through the bushes that hid the opening. The air was fresh, like rare wine after the fear in that tunnel.

We stood in the wood behind the chapel. The moon was climbing over the edge of the hills and there was a tang, a feel of damp in the air.

We started to go, and then Laura stopped dead, eyeing the chapel.

'Come on!' I said, very low in case anybody had come back.

'He's still in there,' she said.

'Alaski? Yes. But if the police have any sense they'll connect it all up the way it really goes—nothing to do with me.'

'I can't leave him there—not like that.'

'This is a hell of a time for sentiment,' I said, furious. 'He's all right. He's in a church, isn't he?'

Women always give me the jumps. Just when you think everything's going well, and you're depending on their reactions, all of a sudden they get as big fools as mules.

'He ought to be in the tomb—where he belongs,' she said.

Surprise shot my anger.

'Is he one of them?' I said.

'A bastard one,' she said. 'But one all the same.'

'He's near enough,' I said. 'They'll put him in there in the end, anyway. Come on.'

Still she hesitated.

'Stone me!' I said. 'You've been honking to get out all night, now the chance is here you stick! What's the matter with you?'

She said nothing. I stuck, too; my reason

272

being superstition. More than once that night her instinct had been ridiculous but right. She could he right again, perhaps.

There was an uneasy quiet under the moon. As far as I was concerned, all the Alaskis were dead, the father, Johnny and Nemo. They had cancelled themselves out.

'Get yourself together,' I said. 'Let's go. It's all tidied up. If the coppers have any sense at all they'll hitch Alaski to Nemo and then they'll fling out the net for Nemo, and they'll never find him because the tunnel fell in with the bang and they won't dig all that out again just in case.'

'All right, then,' she said, in an odd tone.

It made me suspicious, that tone, but I was too impatient to bother about it then.

'Where did the bag go?' she asked as we went through the jungle towards the lodge gates.

I told her.

'Then how will she get away?' Laura said, half stopping in surprise.

'Well, a car, I suppose.'

'But there isn't one. Only the one he took. There's not another one here.'

The sudden vision of slim, elegant Madame Chang footing it over the hills with a half hundredweight bag was so absurd as to be impossible.

'You're wrong, Laura. I've just remembered that Land-Rover. She must have had something worked out,' I said.

She had more worked out than I seriously thought could be true. I don't understand the Orientals any more than I get the drift of the Boot Tricks, but I have heard that they do not concern themselves overmuch with sentiment when they have come to regard themselves as hard done by.

I had the clue to it all then, because I'd heard Madame, but even if she'd explained fully to me in words of one syllable I wouldn't have done anything more than laugh.

'What will she do, then?' Laura persisted.

'Something cunning, like stealing my wagon if we don't hurry!'

We went on down the grassy side of the overgrown drive until the tattered walls of the gate lodge showed up by the reeling network of the rusted gates themselves.

As we came by the open door of the lodge, I grabbed her arm and pulled her into the opening. She had sensed the danger as soon as I had and didn't resist.

In the darkness she hissed : 'Who is it?'

'I don't know. According to my calculations, there shouldn't be anybody left here.'

Listening, I heard soft, quick footfalls on the dusty road outside the gates. There were people in the village, but I couldn't imagine any one of them wandering about at three a.m. without a nefarious reason.

As we listened the footfalls stopped. I signed her to stay still and went and peered round the edge of the door frame. There was a skewed shadow on the ground by the stone gatepost, a dwarf reflection, quite still.

Then I heard a click. It was the kind of click I have heard many times before at the revolver ranges, and I did not like it. It sounded just like somebody checking bullets in a pistol.

The shadow began to move towards the gatepost, slowly, and its head seemed to be sticking out, animal like.

Then I backed into her and pushed her right back into the darkness of the old room.

'Fred!' I whispered.

The human dog came slowly past the lodge, but his animal sense of smell did not seem to be in use then. His whole attention was directed on the way he was going, and twice I saw him stop and look quickly back behind him.

As he went by she tugged my arm.

'But Fred's all right!' she hissed. 'He

wouldn't do anything against me.'

'Why's he here?'

She made no answer.

'He's got a gun,' I said.

'Then he must be after something, because he has nothing here he wants,' she said quickly. 'He just gets money for looking after the place. Part time—'

'Very part time,' I said ironically. 'He—'

But the explanation hit my head and sent a shock of fear down to my feet.

Fred was following somebody.

Which meant somebody we hadn't taken into account had come into these grounds; someone we hadn't seen or heard, but who might have seen or heard us.

But the Merc hadn't come back. We had come down that way from the chapel, and in my state of nerves I had been sure to look all ways, by the front of the house, at the stables where the cars were kept, if any. If the big car had come back I should have seen it.

But according to the list, there had been

only Lucia and Madame in the house. Lucia, I was sure, still bided; Madame, I was equally sure, would have been either in the house or going away from it.

Fred was following somebody who had come in. There couldn't be any mistaking his attitude of the old dog trailer. I had suffered the experience of his art myself, so I knew.

So far as I knew, there was no interested party left in Dead End who would want to come to the Manor at three a.m. and who would rouse the guard dog and his pistol.

'He was following somebody,' I said quietly.

'Will he come back?'

'No guess. Let him move along and we'll dive out of the gate and back to your place—by the woods. I'm not using the road any more between here and the pub. It's too busy.'

I went to the doorway and peered along the drive. Fred had gone, and I didn't hear anything, so I knew he must he walking on the grass.

With Laura breathing almost down my neck, we crept towards the lurching gates, spidery gallows against the moon.

Our way out was simple. We had to get out of the gate, go right alongside the wall, about fifty yards then down the slope amongst the bushes and thence towards the little woods.

Every problem is simple so long as you can get a start to it.

We got to the gates all right, and I got as far as looking through the slanting bars of one gate. It was like looking through a broken harp.

That was as far as we got.

The road stretched out to the inn in a white ribbon under the moon.

About a quarter mile along a black car stood. I stared at it a few seconds to make sure it wasn't moving.

She gave a gasp over my shoulder as I shoved her back.

'The police have come back!' she hissed.

'No,' I said, a crawling starting on my skin. 'It's the Mercedes.'

I felt her shiver against my arm.

The motionlessness of the barouche was queer. Why should it be standing out there in the middle of nowhere when its target was clearly the house?

Suddenly I remembered one thing about the house. The window of Ferdi's room was the only one that looked down the road.

I looked back towards the house. Part of the front could be seen between breaks in the trees, and the window of Ferdi's room—where Lucia was chained to the grate—was flashing light, slowly, irregularly.

There was a floor point on the skirting by the fire. No doubt Lucia had got her foot to it. From the fireplace she could look directly to the road-window and see the car approaching, and so she was signalling it not to come.

For heaven's sake! *Not* to come?

Surely the very thing she needed most was the proximity of her lord, Chang, to undo the iron bracelets that so untimely wed her to the fireplace?

Yet the signal was going out, and the car had stopped, so the sign of the message was clear.

But why in hell should she stop Chang coming back when she should have whooped for joy?

'We can't go out there now,' Laura whispered.

'You're damn right,' I said. 'We'll have to wait till they drive in and get out then.'

'Why are they stopped?' she asked, staring.

'Lucia's stopping them, but she doesn't say why,' I said, pointing to the flashing window. 'Long, slow flashes—the best she can do with her foot.'

As we watched, the light flickered, went red, bloomed for a little, then went out.

'The motor's gone,' Laura said. 'It's an old motor, starts when you switch the light on.'

'Perhaps it was that light attracted Fred,' I said.

I knew I was wrong, but it was a less uncomfortable explanation than the obvious one.

I looked back down the road. The Mercedes, lightless, stayed where it was, a great black cat smiling at a mouse hole.

'Why don't they come?' she breathed. 'I'm scared!'

Under my arm I held the Magog brick, most precious brick in all the world, and the fact that I had it at last merely increased my tension.

It had surely been the unluckiest of all crocks of gold. Since I had tried to find it everything had gone wrong. Death had me by the throat in my first visit; I felt he couldn't be far away now.

'We'll have to wait a bit,' I said. 'They'll come sooner or later.'

I kept watching the Merc, and then the bit of the house that I could see.

Fred went up the main steps. He went slowly, carefully, but his attitude didn't give away any fear.

He stopped at the top and stood there, head wagging slightly.

He was talking to someone I could not see.

Apart from the chained woman, there could have been only Madame and whomever Fred had followed.

Even at that distance I could see Fred's hands, one propping him against the doorpost, the other on his hip. There was no gun, so he had pocketed that.

The person he spoke to was a friend to him.

'Was Fred friendly with Madame Chang?' I asked quietly.

'Fred is a great friend of pretty women,' Laura said. 'He has a little gift for it.'

The Merc stayed still. Fred kept on talking. There was a timelessness about the whole thing that squeezed my heart up so that breathing hurt.

Fred turned on the step, then moved off down to the drive, across that and into the jungle beside it. We waited, listening to him scratching the branches as he drove through to the wall.

There was a silence, then the sounds of pushing through the vegetation again.

Fred appeared on the drive.

'It just stopped up there,' he called. 'No lights and nothing.'

I looked back to the Merc. Somebody got out of it, dived down the slope beside the road and got into the bushes, using the same route as we had planned to do.

'One of them's coming,' she breathed in my ear.

I nodded and shifted Magog under my arm as I stared hard at the big black car. It was difficult to see how many were in it, even if there was anybody at all, the starlight shone so defeatingly on the sloping windscreen.

Fred went up to the top step again. Something was said from the doorway for he turned slowly and looked down towards us on the bend by the lodge.

I comforted myself by thinking whoever was in the doorway could not know we were there. They would not know about the chimney, for the cellar was cut off. They would not know about Magog, for that had never been discovered by them.

Unless Alaski had said something, and that I doubted very much.

I was sure now that Alaski was the real heir to this place, a fact that he had told nobody but Chang, after the failure at Dead End and the flight to Singapore.

That explained Johnny's powerful position in Dead End, the likenesses, the jealous appearance of Nemo, all of it.

Except that for some reason Chang must have thought Alaski dead in Singapore. Perhaps he had organised a killing which had gone wrong and Alaski had turned up unexpectedly to get at the trunk of jewels, which Chang was then looking for.

But Nemo had followed his father. Nemo, also from Singapore, was some kind of believer in Chinese doubling tricks as a sound means of misleading the followers.

Nemo had followed all the way until I had found the treasure and brought it to Laura. Even then he had been foiled because at the very moment he should have taken the bag, he realised that somebody had followed *him*.

That was why he had gone for the gun and not the bag. The gun could have been seen shining in the starlight directly from the window, the bag had been under a table by the wall.

Unlucky Nemo. I felt almost sorry for him.

'It's coming on!'

Fred's voice sounded clearly from the step, and now I saw him turn towards the drive. He brought a pistol from his pocket, checked it again, then put it back and stood waiting.

A blaze of light, yellow against the moonglow, swept the house front, jazzing it with the heavy black shadows of trees.

The Mercedes was on its way, lights on.

Which also meant the creeping vanguard from the bushes must have reached us.

I gripped Laura's arm tightly.

'Don't move at all,' I whispered, then got my gun in my free hand.

CHAPTER X

I

The big black car came in at the gate very slowly, very quietly, sneaking round, like a prowling animal. As it passed the gates it went even slower, and suddenly the lights went out. More like a cat now it came on close to where we hid in the shadows. It stopped, the motor whispering. Then even that whisper stopped.

I felt Laura shiver under my grip. The near door of the Merc opened but nobody got out.

'Mr. Blake.'

Chang's voice was smooth and high as ever, bland and as lacking in emotion as his olive face, but he didn't show it now.

He knew I was there, he spoke so low, so

normally. He wasn't calling. He just knew I was there. I gestured Laura to stay where she was, gave her Magog and went out of the shadows to the car.

'Come in, Mr. Blake,' Chang said.

My gun was in my pocket. I kept my hand on it and got in beside the driver. He was slumped like a great sack in the seat staring ahead to the bit of the house he could see beyond the bend in the jungle.

'I have been making enquiries, Mr. Blake,' he said, without looking at me. 'And I believe that the development which you had in mind for this place was no more than the removal of a certain collection.'

'I'm not a collector,' I said.

'I am,' Chang said, still without emotion. 'Let me explain a little to you and then it is possible that you may help me in my difficulty.'

'Do that,' I said.

'I am, you see, a lawyer,' Chang said. 'But people come to me not so much to be defended, or to prosecute but to have me find things out that they wish to know, or perhaps things that they have lost. Perhaps, even they wish to find things which do not belong to them.'

'And when Alaski came to you, what did he want you to find?' I said.

'He did not come as Alaski,' said Chang. 'It was I found out who he was and why he was East. You know, as I do now, that Alaski fled because things here had gone wrong. It was not till after he had got away that he heard Johnny was dead. It seems that evidence had been so arranged here that Johnny would be left free of any charge against him. That is to say his safety had been previously bought, and it was thought that you and your friends had died in the explosion in the mine gallery.'

'A reasonable assumption,' I said. 'But wrong.'

'Some years back, Alaski had amassed a small fortune in jewellery, come I know not how, but it was hidden here and formed the capital upon which his later success was founded. He used part of it here, part there—' Chang shrugged, '—money makes money, so they say, but certainly it attracts itself. But it also attracts greed. Alaski was such a man, wanting more riches, more power, more mystery.

'When you beat him, Mr. Blake, you took away from him all those precious things. He meant to get them back, but even more than that he meant to get you.'

It was dead quiet in the car. I could feel the chill of October creeping in the night.

'He knew you would come back here,' Chang went on. 'And so I was commissioned to come here and openly become the agent for this estate, and to wait for you.'

'But surely you had to find the collection, too?'

Chang laughed softly.

'But no, Mr. Blake. He knew very well where that was.'

There was a pause and I felt the chill even more though my fingers were sticky on the gun.

'Unfortunately, Alaski was far from a trusting man,' said Chang and sighed. 'His patience became strained too far and he risked coming back. Perhaps he did not feel the hiding place of the collection was secure.'

'So he re-hid it—in Johnny's coffin,' I said.

Chang nodded askance.

'So? It was there? It was ironic, then, that Lucia should have used the vault to hide Alaski!'

'He was claustrophobic,' I said.

Chang stared ahead.

'It was hoped that some hours in solitary meditation might cause him to reveal where the collection was,' he said.

'You were after it yourself?'

He shook his head.

'No. But my staff found themselves unable to resist the call of so much. They were in the first place selected for their efficiency and curious knowledge rather than their honesty. It played back at me, you understand, as such things will. I was safe with them until they found, somehow, about the collection. I came to know what they were doing, even that they had put Alaski to consider his future. They did not think that someone had come here who would not wish him to tell at all.'

'Alaski was hanged tonight,' I said. 'So he couldn't have said where the stuff was anyhow.'

Chang just nodded. He didn't seem surprised or shocked by the news. It seemed to me that what he was saying was a mixture of fact and surmise scrambled for continuity.

'There was another son,' Chang said. 'It was one of my discoveries. Once I began to study Alaski, you understand, I began to find so many things. It was like cutting the top from an anthill.'

'Alaski was a war pilot,' I said.

'Yes, that, I believe, is how the collection was brought in.'

'From what you say, this collection was his be-all and end-all?' I asked. I wanted to know about Magog.

Chang considered. I felt he was playing some mental game.

'I would not be sure about that,' he said after a while. 'Often I felt there was something more, but I have no real evidence. It could have been just an idea, or a misreading of Alaski's self-assurance. I do not know.'

I glanced towards the darkness of the bushes where Laura would be, holding Magog to her frightened bosom.

'Well, so this is the end of the little treasure hunt,' I said. 'I've lost. I'd better get on with my developing.'

'How can you have lost, Mr. Blake?' Chang looked round at me.

'Because Madame Chang has the collection, and I am sure you will see that she keeps it.'

Chang's face hardened in surprise. The reflection of moonlight off the car made his black eyes seem bright as shoe leather.

'She has it?' he said.

'She has. It passed through several hands, but she has it now.'

'Tell me how you know this?' he said.

'I listened at a door,' I said and told him what I had heard climbing the flue.

'And you just let her take it?' said Chang smoothly.

'I don't say I just let it go,' I said. 'But I had to think carefully and while I was doing that I looked out and saw your motor car anchored in the roads.'

'I saw you behind the gate,' Chang said. He put his hand down to a pair of binoculars lying on the seat between us. 'I sent Ferdi on. He signalled you were still there when I drove in. There is no magic.'

I began to wonder what he was waiting for. His lack of emotion, his odd quietness were so strange that they chilled more than any threat.

Yet I had the feeling of a sadness somewhere in this quiet face.

'Somebody phoned the police from here,' I said.

'There's no phone,' he said.

'That's what the man said,' I mocked him. 'But it was done. There should have been your wife and the secretary here, but it was a man who spoke. The line goes up from here over the hill, right away from the village. And somebody saw in the window of the pub. You have the long distance eyes right by you now.'

'I have not the figure for climbing poles.'

'Ferdi has. Ferdi's all sorts of a mechanic. With these naval type eyes you could read the label on a beer bottle at a thousand yards. He could see in that room.'

Chang nodded.

'You reason well,' he said. 'And Ferdi did not go with me to London. I picked him up on my way just now.'

'And Ali?"

'He came with me. I dropped him outside. I wanted to speak with you.'

'So the two thugs are just outside the wall here.'

'They will wait.'

'Why did you want to tell me all this?'

'I believe that you can help.'

'But how? You know it all. More than I do.'

'You came twice to this place,' he said. 'The first time things went wrong for you, and you did not get what you wanted for you came back. Once more your journey is difficult and dangerous, yet still you stay. There is a treasure which you find, and which you hear is in the hands of a woman, yet you leave it.'

'I saw your car.'

'There is one other thing, one secret thing, lost these twenty years or more and may be anywhere in the world. All that long time ago, when the war was still burning in Asia, a piece was stolen from a temple, by whom, no one knows. The Japanese, the Chinese, the Gurkhas, the Indians, the Americans—the English? Who can say? But it was a piece more precious than the world has known. Today, throughout the world, there are five men who would compete in secrecy to buy it. The price? Three, four, five million sterling? Who knows? The seller? He would be safe. The buyer would never tell on him.'

He shifted his great bulk in the seat. I felt the sweat icing on my face.

'For years I have been trying to find what became of that piece, but the smoke of war makes all things uncertain,' Chang said. 'But then Alaski came, and his story roused my interest again. His fortune had been taken from the East, by whatever means and smuggled into England. He had the means, he could have been at the temple.

'Now see me here. The fortune which he

spoke of was worth, after he had used so much, perhaps a quarter million sterling. Good, but not vast. Yet Alaski's ideas were bigger, much bigger than that. They would require much more capital, but due to his crimes, he had lost all his means but the treasure at Dead End. Treasure of that kind is easy to sell, even though the price is only a percentage.

'How, then would one sell such a piece as I have in my mind? One must know the half-dozen secret men who would buy, and who would have the money to buy. So that whoever was to sell must have the connections.

'With Alaski I saw a politician, a minister, with connections with the great of all nations with usable currency. The mist began to clear a little and to come into the shape that I wanted.

'There was another side to Alaski. He had a weak heel. He had many mistresses. I make it my business when I come here to investigate his love affairs, one by one, very patiently. It takes time, but in the end it is done.

'And I find that among these ladies there is one, a hard, fair girl perhaps by the name of Jane?' He did not look at me but went on staring at the strip of house front.

'There are many Janes,' I said.

'But this one I find moves on. She leaves Alaski and becomes the love of a Mr. Jonathan Blake, of whom you will have heard.

'Now it is possible that in such intimacy, a lady might come to know or suspect that which the man might well think he has safely hidden. Jane could have found that Alaski was contacting secret and rich men outside the political world. She might have wondered why. She might have pursued the same thread of thought as my humble brain has done. She might have enlisted your help, for she would need a man of some courage and quickness, some shrewdness and experience in dangerous work. She might have chosen you after she had loved you, and then gone back to Alaski so as to be brought by him to Dead End, where she knew there was really a more valuable treasure than the collection of jewellery which, for psychological reasons, Alaski was not all that careful to keep hidden.'

He sat back in the seat. I said nothing. There was nothing that could be said with advantage.

'So Mr. Blake, we arrive at Dead End in reality,' Chang said.

'Too damn right, we had. He knew it all, the fat beast, yet still he seemed sad about it.'

'I waited for you to find the hiding place,' said Chang. 'But in time I realised you did not know it. You had only an area, a locality that you had to search. That is what I believed, and so I decided to go to London and prove your link with Jane, and to leave you to make your search.'

'Supposing I had got away with it—if I'd found whatever it is?'

'Ferdi was left to watch. And Lucia. She is clever.'

'Not clever enough,' I said.

'Where is—the piece?' he said, and looked at me fully.

'If I had it, I would have gone,' I said. There was no longer point in pretending I didn't know about it.

'Why did you not go when you had the collection?'

'Because I didn't know where it came from. It could have been hot enough to jug me for years. I don't want that kind of merchandise.'

'But the other is so safe,' Chang murmured.

I shrugged and wondered what the hell Laura was doing out in the still darkness. Maybe she could hear us, in which case she might go with the little box tucked under her arm. Except she wouldn't know how to sell it.

Behind me were Ferdi and Ali, and ahead of me was Fred with his pistol and right at my thigh was Chang of whom I began to get the weird idea that in hunting Magog he was fighting for some mystic honour of the East, for which murder would merely be a necessary sacrifice.

'It has a code name—Magog,' I said. 'Did you come just because of that?'

'When Alaski came it stirred the mists of the years,' Chang said. 'For all of twenty years we have searched and then suddenly, with this wicked man there seemed to come a little ray in the darkness. Now it is a bright, shining light. I have succeeded in the one good work of my life.'

Dedicated. My heart sank. With normal greed and dishonesty I am at home. With dedication I am at sea. I never can quite believe in it. Watching Chang then I felt there was something up his sleeve.

Something caught my eye. I could just see shadows in the rearview mirror. Ferdi and Ali were coming up to the car from behind.

'Give Magog to me,' Chang said softly.

'If I had it I wouldn't,' I said.

Something moved ahead of us, passing between bushes on the bend. The sound of an engine broke out. Chang lifted his head.

'It's the Land-Rover!' I said.

The truck came towards us, cutting the bend, its engine muttering, no lights showing. There was something strangely horrible about it and for a moment I did not see why.

Then suddenly the moon shone brightly on it as it passed a break in the trees and I saw what was wrong.

There was no driver.

I barged Chang at the same instant he opened his door, and he went out. 'Run!' I yelled, and recoiled so that I went out of my own door.

I made a good fall on my feet, knees bent and sprang off again into the bushes. It was instinct perhaps, or in the instant of death my poor old brain connected up all the things I knew, but I ran hard.

The Land-Rover ground into the front of the Merc and then for the second time that night my eyeballs were seared by a flash. Blast took me forward off my feet and I went head first, arms trying to protect my face, into the tangle of the undergrowth.

How I landed I don't know, nor felt anything, for the roar of the explosion took away all senses but that of a thumping pain in the ear drums and I just lay in the bed of twigs and prickles and let the flame pass over. I was hit several times by bits and felt glad my face was down.

The world died into stillness, but there was smoke and the brilliance of flame that was too hot to flicker. I looked back. The vehicles, locked together, were burning. In the flames I saw bodies lying round them, but they didn't move.

Madame Chang had scored for the years of humiliation. I was the only one of four left from the holocaust.

As I got up I looked around into the

brilliantly lit nightmare scene of the wood round me. I did not see Laura. I did not see anybody alive.

'Laura! Laura!' I broke through the jungle towards the gate. When I got there I called again, but no one answered.

The road outside was empty. I ran back towards the house, keeping in the bushes to avoid having to see the sprawling men on the ground. There wasn't any point in seeing them. They couldn't look like that and be alive. Madame must have filled the Land-Rover with sticks of that left-over dynamite.

In my somewhat shaken calculations then, Fred and Madame remained in the house ahead of me, or at best, had just run. Fred might be useful to her. He could know a way through the hills where the police wouldn't go.

My one idea then was to find Laura and clear out. I called a couple of times as I went slowly through the undergrowth, looking all ways, and cheated by the shivering shadows thrown by the fire.

Soon that fire would be seen from way off and the police would be back.

Then I saw something move ahead of me, something down in the tall spiky grass.

'Laura!'

She was struggling to get up when I got to her.

'Are you all right?'

She just gasped a bit and clung to me, shivering. 'Take me away,' she whispered. 'Now!'

I got her up.

'Where's the box?'

She shook her head.

'The box—' She looked vaguely round then started. 'There's a fire!'

'Hell with the fire!' I said. 'Where's that box?'

'I was knocked over—' She wiped a hand over her dirty face.

'You've lost the torch, too, for God's sake!' I said, pushing her away from me.

'We haven't got long. Beat the grass around. I must have that box!'

We beat the grass and there was nothing. The leaping fire threw jazzing shadows, long one second, short the next. You couldn't make out what was what, with the jagged stripy shadows of the young trees dancing about, and the bushes jagging along the grass.

'You fell there. You could have thrown it when you fell. Let's poke. Come on, Laura. On this line.'

We poked and pushed with sticks and our feet, but we couldn't find Magog.

Then we heard the police gong trilling in the night behind the cracking and hissing of the fire.

'Get out of it!' I said, grabbing her hand. 'Quick!'

We ran, over the drive and into the jungle, through that and came out to the chapel. The chapel was the obvious place, for it had the vault, too. But it was going to be a long hide. There was enough work for the police to keep them around for days, except they would almost certainly get Madame and Fred before the night was out.

I opened the old chapel door and shoved Laura in. There was a blaze of white light sweeping the trees, cutting through the red glare and the great pillar of black smoke reaching for the moon. I closed the door and we stayed in the ruddy darkness. The fire reached through the little stained glass windows way up the old stone walls. Why they had iron barred them, I never knew unless church robbers had once been great scalers.

We heard voices out in the night, human voices and the crackle of the radiophone promising reinforcements. At first, I suppose it would look like an accident, and be a little while before they grasped what a bang it had been.

As I put the bar across the old doors I thought I heard the lock grate. It gave me a turn so that my heart stopped, but no other sound came from outside the panels.

'My nerves are jumping,' I said.

We went down the aisle.

'You don't have to look,' I said as we came near Alaski. 'Just watch the back of my neck.'

She must have shut her eyes for she got my waistband again and I towed her into the vestry. I went down to the other door and then unmistakably, the lock groaned.

Someone was outside, locking us in.

I waited a moment, then a small, harsh horrible voice said something and trailed off into a croaking.

It was the mechanical parrot Nemo had used to answer the speaking tube from wherever he had hidden. I realised we hadn't even found that place.

There was a pause, then a voice I knew too well.

'Goodbye, Johnny,' it said. 'I'll always remember you, darling.'

There was a little laugh and then silence.

'Janey!' I said, and swallowed.

It's a long wait. Police are still roaming round the grounds and I suppose we should be thankful it looks, from the outside, as if the church has been locked up for years. I know because we've heard them say so and pass on.

So we're safe from them, locked in, but when they've gone, how do we get out?

As I said at the start, I shouldn't have come back. It's done no good. There were so many other things I could have done.

I suppose this is the first diary ever written on a parish register, but it has a lot of pages never likely to be used for the usual stuff.

It's surprising how far a ball point goes on.

Specially when you're hungry. Everything goes on endlessly.

I love Laura.

I'm glad.

It looks as if she's all I've got left.

The publishers hope that this book has given you enjoyable reading. Large Print Books are especially designed to be as easy to see and hold as possible. If you wish a complete list of our books, please ask at your local library or write directly to: Dales Large Print Books, Long Preston, North Yorkshire, BD23 4ND, England.

This Large Print Book for the Partially sighted, who cannot read normal print, is published under the auspices of

THE ULVERSCROFT FOUNDATION

THE ULVERSCROFT FOUNDATION

. . . we hope that you have enjoyed this Large Print Book. Please think for a moment about those people who have worse eyesight problems than you . . . and are unable to even read or enjoy Large Print, without great difficulty.

You can help them by sending a donation, large or small to:

**The Ulverscroft Foundation,
1, The Green, Bradgate Road,
Anstey, Leicestershire, LE7 7FU,
England.**

or request a copy of our brochure for more details.

The Foundation will use all your help to assist those people who are handicapped by various sight problems and need special attention.

Thank you very much for your help.

Other DALES Mystery Titles In Large Print

PHILIP McCUTCHAN
Assignment Andalusia

PETER CHAMBERS
Don't Bother To Knock

ALAN SEWART
Dead Man Drifting

PETER ALDING
Betrayed By Death

JOHN BEDFORD
Moment In Time

Other DALES Mystery Titles
In Large Print

PETER CHAMBERS
Somebody Has To Lose

PETER ALDING
A Man Condemned

ALAN SEWART
Plight Of The Innocents

RODERIC JEFFRIES
The Benefits Of Death

MARY BRINGLE
Murder Most Gentrified